一定要讓你發表得出去之

英文科技論文便覽

楊勝安 博士 編著

全華圖書股份有限公司 印行

Contents 目錄

中國工業職業教育學會
獎　　狀

楊勝安　先生參加本會 95 年度優良工職教育人員金鐸獎選拔，經評審榮獲　研究獎　特頒此狀，以資鼓勵

理事長　孟繼洢

中華民國 95 年 12 月 16 日

Preface 序言

　　台灣近幾年來，高等科技研究所如雨後春筍般設立，甚至研究型大學研究生人數已然超過大學生人數；然而這期間研究生的英文科技寫作水準卻未跟著提昇；指導教授們常望著堆積的研究生論文與研究成果，無暇改成英文稿而興嘆。身為指導教授的我們，偶而遇到英文好之研究生並能寫英文稿，頓然輕鬆許多，但是往往可遇不可求。筆者任教科技大學，更深深地體會這一點無奈！

　　由於SCI、Ei與SSCI的篇數被列為大學之研究能力表現之指標，同時也是國家競爭力一項參考指標，因此國外大學科技英文寫作課相當被重視，也有不少相關科技英文寫作之書籍出版，包括日本此方面的書，國內亦有人翻譯；獨獨我們國內科技學者，自行編輯科技英文寫作之書，卻屬鳳毛麟角！

　　科技論文之英文語法，並不等同於傳統英文所要求之語法；前者著重簡潔、有效、清楚表達，後者卻注重文辭優美。科技英文比較講究適合與否，縱使語法沒錯。而所謂適合語法，是大部份英美學者所表現方式。例如，科技論文建議使用主動語態，較屬簡潔、有效表達；然而持續使用第一人稱：「I」或「We」，又顯得不夠含蓄，因此改成第三人稱較適宜，亦即用「The present paper or articles or study」當

主詞。事實上，SCI、Ei等科技論文為強調研究行為或結果而當主詞時，常常採用被動語態。足見直接從SCI、Ei等摘錄常用句型，是個有效對策，就像套用理工學科公式一樣的好用。筆者研究生（科技大學）循此模式已成功發表在SCI、Ei級期刊五篇以上（兩年內），參見筆者著作目錄（2004～05）。套句廣告用詞「相信我，你（的學生）也做得到！」（Trust me! You can make it！）

在完成書面報告篇之際，又接到2005年在波蘭舉行國際熱傳研討會指定筆者為分組主持人（session chairman），有點惶恐與緊張，但也是種肯定筆者研究之榮譽。雖然近年來，在國內也主持過數場研討會，但是面對各國口音，仍戰戰兢兢。因此，決定收集參予國際研討會實際經驗與製作Power Point技巧，一併納入本書第三篇，同時於附錄中放置投稿篇與研討會實例之光碟，方便教師上課使用參考。祈盼此舉可拋磚引玉。

基本上，本書是為科技英文報告而編輯，適合理工科同學。值得你擺一本在身旁，並隨時再添加入漂亮實用句型於筆記欄。最後，為了個人指導之研究生與今年捨台大電機系進入交大菁英班之兒子竣宇舖路，再度野人獻曝此一便覽。由於筆者才疏學淺，疏漏之處在所難免，尚祈海內外學者先進不吝指正，是幸！願以此書獻給我的家人。

2007識于澄清湖

壹

科技寫作與文法篇

一、科技寫作通則

1. 科技論文力求簡明、扼要，故儘量使用簡潔有力單一字，少用兩個字以上同義詞語。

避免；少用為宜	較簡潔有效字	避免；少用為宜	較簡潔有效字
a large number of	Several（or many）	In spite of the fact that	Although
a small number of	few	On a regular basis	Regularly
a majority of	most	take into consideration	consider
as a result of	because	bring to a conclusion	conclude
smaller in size	smaller	It is evident that	Evidently,
has the ability to	can	It is clear that.	Clearly,..
lacks the ability to	cannot	make assumption	assume
make changes in	change	It would appear that	Apparently,
There is no doubt but that	Unquestionably,	Owing to the fact that	Seeing that; Because

避免；少用為宜	較簡潔有效字	避免；少用為宜	較簡潔有效字
it is often the case that	often	is a requirement of	require
as a consequence of	because	in most cases	usually; mostly
in order to	to	in the even that	if
due to the fact that	Because	In the vicinity of	near
in view of the fact that	Because	In connection with	about
in a careful manner	carefully	It may well be that	Perhaps,

◎ 科技論文為求簡明，若能用一個動詞表示，就不要使用由名詞與介係詞組成同義的片語。如下面諸例，以第一個動詞為較佳。

assign = perform an assignment of

conclude = draw a conclusion

calibrate = perform calibration of

discover = make a discovery

experiment with = conduct an experiment on

simulate = perform simulation

examine = perform an examination of

investigate = undertake an investigation of

improve = make（achieve）an improvement

provide = make a provision of

recommend = make a recommendation

reserve = make a reservation of

review thoroughly = make a thorough review of

2. 科技論文為求有效表達，儘量使用主動語態少用被動語態：（Passive writing has traditionally been used in scientific writing, but active writing is now preferred by many editors.）好的寫作，儘量以主動語態，偶而穿插一些被動語態即可。不過若主詞為作者本人，為求含蓄，避免多次提到作者本人，反而用被動語態較妥，或者以「This （The present） study」；「This paper or work」；「The present article」當主詞；亦即避免太常出現「I...」或「We...」。

例如：本研究使用一創新方法解決了棘手問題。

This study applies a novel approach to solve the tough problem.

（有效表達）

In this study, we apply a novel approach to solve the tough problem.

（較差）

例如：本文比較此方法的優、缺點以求選出一個合適的。

This paper compares the advantages and disadvantages of the methods to select an appropriate one.

◎ 其實，有些研究術語當主詞時，可採主動，例如：

（1） This project attempts to...

本計畫嘗試……

（2） This investigation reviews...

本調查回顧……

（3） The present approach considers...

本方法探討……

（4） The proposed procedure identifies...

本擬定步驟意指……

（5） The present method can effectively determine...

本方法可有效解決……

（6） This method suggested using...

本方法建議使用……

（7）The following section describes (discusses; summarizes; outlines)...

下一個階段描述（討論；總結；概述）……

（8）The following equation assumes...

下列方程式假設……

（9）The proposed procedure implements related tasks of...

本擬定步驟完成……的相關工作

（10）The experiment determined how... affects...

本實驗決定出……如何影響……

◎ 練習改善下列被動語態句子

（1）The assumptions made during the simulation study were...

（2）In this section, the effects of information source errors on the behavior of the system are explored.

（3）It can be seen from observation of the results that...

（4）It can be seen from the present data that...

（5）In this study, it was discovered that...

（6）Based on these results, it appears that...

（7）An increase in abundance of water is noticed going up this area.

Ans:

(1) The simulation study assumes that...

(2) This section explores the effects of information source errors on the behaviorof the system.

(3) The results indicate (=demonstrate) that...

(4) The present data show that...

(5) This study discovered that...

(6) These results suggest that...

(7) Water increase in abundance upwards through this area.

另外有些特殊情況亦使用被動語態：

（1）強調動作（研究成果）而非作者，或授與動作者不明；有時論文研究者只以文獻號碼代表時，例如：在文獻回顧的論文。

（2）欲保持在整個段落同一主題連貫性時。（To keep the subject and focus consistent throughout a passage.）

例如：這些過程有一點被誤解。

The procedures were somehow misinterpreted.

被動：Territory size was found to vary with population density.

領土的大小被發現隨著人口密度而變動。

主動：Territory size varied with population density.

（某人發現）領土的大小隨著人口密度而變動。

3. 有些誇飾程度性之修飾語，在科技寫作較無意義應盡量避免，例如： very、quite、rather、completely 與 totally 等。建議，改成像 significantly等。

4. 科技論文常出現「issue」、「matter」、「subject」、「topic」等，表示「議題、課題、主題」四個字，注意分辨真正意義：

（1）「issue」（引起辯論的問題、議題）：a political issue（政治性的議題）。

（2）「matter」（思考議題、事務）：a matter of great concern

（3）「subject」（主題、課題）：an interesting subject of conversation（有興趣話題）

（4）「topic」（主要論點、主題）：a research topic arisen（引人研究的主題）

5. 科技論文常出現混淆使用「affect」與「effect」。當動詞時，更容易混淆。

（1）Affect 影響：Smoking may affect your health.

（2）effect造成：Smoking may effect （=lead to） change in your health.

（3）affect =influence=exert an effect （influence） on

6. 請記得在「i.e.」與「e.g.」之後加逗號 「，」成「i.e.,」與「e.g.,」

7. 若你舉例，「for example」或「like」，請不要在其後以「etc.」結束。

8. 文獻回顧時，請注意正確使用標點，例如：「Smith et al. [1] shows」，而非「Smith et. al. shows.」。

9. 請記得在「respectively」之前加逗號而成「, respectively.」。

10. 相關的研究或文獻為「related work or literature」， 而非「related works or literatures」

11. 使用Figures show, depict, indicate, illustrate, demonstrate，而非「refer to Fig. 1」。

12. 「At the same time」：涉及兩件事同時發生，但稍有相反論點表「然而」意思。The results have been disappointing. At the same time the research is in its infancy.

研究結果一直令人失望，不過研究是處在起步階段。

13. 科技論文中，常見描述兩參數或變數間互為消長關係：

（1）Y 隨 X 增加而增加：

Y increases with X.

=Y increases （= rises or goes up） with an increase in X.

=Y increases with increasing X.

= Y goes up as X increases.

◎ 隨 …… 而增加一點：to increase a little with

◎ 增加或減少2%：increase or decrease by 2%

（2） Y隨 X 增加而減少：

Y decreases （= declines or reduces） with an increase in X.

（3） 當 X 增加時，Y幾乎保持定值（常數）：

Y remains approximately constant (= is nearly uniform) as X

increases.

① Y強烈（明顯）地受到 X 變化而定（或影響）

Y is strongly (significantly = greatly = markedly) dependent on

（= affected by = influenced by） X.

= X affects （= influences） Y to a large extent.

（較上式簡潔有效）

其他程度性：Y輕微地受到X影響：

X affects Y a little (= to a small extent)

幾乎不受影響：to be almost unaffected by

② Y 與 X 具有強烈（明顯）地關係。

Y is closely（= highly = significantly）related to X.

其他程度性副詞：不明顯地（insignificantly）；微乎其微地

或可忽視地（negligibly）；有幾分地、些許地或可察覺地

（appreciably）。

③ Y 與 X 具有比例關係：

Y 與 X 成正（反）比：Y is directly（inversely）proportional

to X.

Y 與 X 的兩次方成正（反）比：Y is directly（inversely）

proportional to the square of X.

14. 主詞與動詞在人稱上或單複數需注意一致性：

A survey of... ；A combination of... ；A list of... ；A brief description of...

；a review of... 等為主詞，使用單數動詞；其他重要例子，Ving（動名

詞片語）當主詞使用單數動詞。

「（某文獻）最近對於探討……的問題作一個完整的回顧」

A comprehensive review of problems concerned with... has been given

recently by [Ref.]

（1）literature、evidence、information、software、hardware、

equipment、attention、research 等，只有單數。

（2）various methods、differential temperatures、data與criteria必用複數動詞。

15. 轉折用語與片語（Transitional Words and Phrases）

科技論文相當重視起承轉合，使用轉折用語或連接性副詞與片語，來連接由一觀念進入另一觀念之平順。底下列出常見轉折用語與片語：

（1）表示原因與結果（cause and effect）：

所以：consequently, therefore, accordingly, as a result

因此：hence, thus

因為：because, for this reason

（2）「既然那樣」：in that case, in such circumstances, such being the case, under such circumstances

例如：我很遺憾你生病了。既然如此，你可以放假一天。

I am sorry that you are ill. In such circumstances, you may take the day off.

（3）次序sequence：若只有兩點陳述可採用「再者」：further、furthermore、in addition (=Additionally)、moreover、besides；若有三點或以上陳述可採用分項陳述即第一點、第二點……最後。

第一點：firstly；第二點：secondly；最後：finally。

◎ 注意：若有涉及時間先後，使用「Firstly、Then、Next (Afterwards)、Finally （More recently）」亦可用「First、Second、Third...」。

例如：本問題有三方面必須陳述

There are three aspects of this problem have to be addressed.

第一個問題是關於……

The first question involves...

第二個問題是關於……

The second problem relates to...

第三個方面是探討……

The third aspect deals with...

（4） 表示比較（comparison）或比照（contrast）：

類似、相似地：similarly, in the same way, likewise, in like manner

然而：however, nevertheless, nonetheless, even so

相反地、對比之下：in contrast = by contrast

與NP對比：in contrast with + NP

比較之下：in comparison, in comparison with + NP,

compared with + NP；compared to + NP （比喻為）

相反地：on the contrary, conversely

與NP相反：contrary to + NP

否則：otherwise

但是：but

另一方面：On the other hand

（5）例如：for example, for instance

譬如說：like + NP, such as, such ~ as

（6）尤其是像……的東西或人：notably, especially, particularly, in particular

（7）因此（為了……目的）：for this purpose, for this reason, to this end, with this object

（8）就某人所知：as far as one knows, to one's knowledge, to one's understanding

其他類似：

① 令人驚奇地：to one's surprise

② 令人欣喜：to one's delight

③ 令人遺憾：to one's... regret

（9）一般而言：In general, Generally speaking, On the whole, All in all, as a（general）rule, Broadly speaking, Overall

大體上說來：In most cases, as usual (= usually)，as a rule, more often than not

在某種程度上來說：in a sense, to some extent, to a certain extent, to a... degree

嚴格來說：strictly speaking

簡單地說：to put the matter simply

（10）不管怎樣：anyway, anyhow, in any case, after all, at any rate

（11）表示「強調」的轉折，即「誠然……但是」：{indeed, admittedly, no doubt, unquestionably, It is true （that）, to be sure} + {but or yet}+ S+V

（12）也就是說：that is, in other words, namely, this means, "i.e.,"

（13）用於結論表示「總之」：in a word, in summary, to sum up；

「簡而言之」：In short, to be brief, in brief, to put it briefly

（14）如前提及或所述：As mentioned before, As has been stated, ；

如上述提及：as mentioned above, as referenced above

（15）表示贊同的，如「無疑」、「不可否認地」、「的確」：

certainly, indeed, undeniably, without any question, truly

（16）表示「由於」的介系詞片語或副詞片語

Due to 與 Owing to（or Because of）的對照用法。

Due to，補述用法：This invention is due to Edison。

Losses due to preventable fires are unforgettable.

Due to 不可像「Owing to」或「Because of」的副詞用法置於句首。

He lost his first game, owing to （because of = on account of）carelessness.

（17）表示「在當時」、「在此期間」：In the mean time, Meanwhile

16. 為求較美修辭表現，要注意文章結構的平行對稱。只要有多項以對等連接如 and、or、but 並列；或者 both... and... 、either... or... 、not（only）... but （also）... 不管是主詞動詞或補語均要注意結構的平行對稱；亦採用同樣之詞類，例如：

（1）選擇適當的值與變動相關參數可達成最佳結果。

Selecting an appropriate value of X and varying the related parameters can achieve the optimal results.

（2）這項革新使機器便於移動、不易故障、耐用。

This innovation makes the machine easy to move, free of trouble and durable.（此句用法不佳，不具平行對稱，改成下句具有平行對稱用法較佳）

This innovation makes the machine movable, reliable, and durable.

（3）鑽石因美麗、耐久與稀有，而有價值。

Diamond is valued for its beauty, durability, and because it is rare.

（此句用法不佳，不具平行對稱，改成下句具有平行對稱用法較佳。）

Diamond is valued for its beauty, durability, and rarity.

（4）科技論文中，分項敘述（條例示）時，例如：陳列假設條件、數值計算步驟、實驗步驟，甚至條例結論，使用平行對稱結構較佳。

（5）另外，進行比較時亦使用對等詞性，如「... , rather than... 」（……，而不是……）：

運動學是探討物體如何移動而不關切爲何運動。

Kinematics is concerned with how bodies move rather than why they move.

（6）其他 First、First of all 要配合 Second、Third；至於，Firstly 配合 Secondly、Thirdly、……、Finally。

17. 變化句子結構種類，避免持續簡單句：

在文章內持續使用「主詞＋動詞＋受詞」的簡單句易使人覺得單調無趣。時而換成複合句（Complex sentence）、集合句（Compound sentence）或混合句（Compound-complex sentence），比較有多變性。

茲分述這四種句子如下：

（1）只由一個主要句子形成，而不含任何其他子句如對等子句，或從屬子句者，稱爲簡單句。

（2）由兩個或兩個以上的對等子句而成的句子，稱之爲集合句。集合句通常用對等連接詞and、or、but、for、so、otherwise（否則）……，連接這些對等子句。結構大致如下：

主詞＋動詞＋……＋（and, or, but, for, so, otherwise）＋主詞＋動詞＋……。

（3）由一個主要子句與一個或一個以上的從屬子句組合而成的句子，稱爲複合句。複合句通常用從屬連接詞（包括關係代名詞與關係副詞）that、if、though、because、since、before、as、whether、when、while、still、until、unless、as soon as、no sooner... than、so... that、such... that、lest... should、in order that... may、even if、than、where、why、how、who、whom、whose、which、what...等連接這些子句。結構大致如下：

主詞＋動詞＋……＋（that, if, as, when, because, unless, though...）＋主詞＋動詞＋……。

（4）主要子句與從屬子句的位置可以調換，從屬子句有時被放在主要子句的中間。

（5）在集合句的任一個或每一個對等子句中，另外附有從屬子句的句子，稱之爲混合句。混合句結構大致如下：

對等子句＋（從屬子句）＋對等連接詞＋對等子句＋從屬子句。

18. 簡單句依動詞的性質來分類可分成五種基本句型：

（1）　1st type：S（主詞）＋V（動詞）

（2）　2nd type：S（主詞）＋V（動詞）＋C（補語）

（3）　3rd type：S（主詞）＋V（動詞）＋O（受詞）

（4）　4th type：S（主詞）＋V（動詞）＋O1（受詞）＋O2（受詞）

（5）　5th type：S（主詞）＋V（動詞）＋O（受詞）＋C（補語）

茲分述如下：

（1）　主詞＋完全不及物動詞

The flow separation occurs.

The great ending appears.

（2）　主詞＋不完全不及物動詞＋（主詞）補語

It sounds good.

You become a graduate student.

（3）　主詞＋完全及物動詞＋受詞

We conducted a research project.

Professor Wang wrote a report.

（4）　主詞＋與格動詞＋（間接）受詞＋（直接）受詞

I give you a lecture.

I teach you English.

（5） 主詞＋不完全及物動詞＋受詞＋（受詞）補語

I elected Mr. Chen President.

He made us faithful.

19. 所謂複合句由從屬連接詞所引導的子句，依其功用可分成副詞子句、

形容詞子句與名詞子句。

副詞從屬子句大致有：（1）表示因果、目的關係的副詞子句；（2）

表示條件的副詞子句；（3）表示讓步的副詞子句；（4）表示比較的

副詞子句；（5）表示時間與地方的副詞子句，分別說明如下：

（1） 表示因果、目的關係的副詞子句：

首先是表示原因與理由，較常使用從屬連接詞Because（因為）

或 since（既然）。

　Because S + V +... ; S + V +... （主要子句）

　S + V +... （主要子句）since S + V +...

如果主要子句與從屬子句具有同一個主詞應改用介系詞片語：

Because of ＋名詞（或動名詞）或 Owing to （= Thanks to, Due

to） ＋名詞（或動名詞）較簡潔。

表示結果：so... that... 、such... that... ；如此……以致於……。

表示目的：... in order that... may（or might）為求（為要達

成）……。

（2） 表示條件的副詞子句：分成肯定與否定條件。

肯定：If + S + V...（如果……）, S + V +...（主要子句）。

S＋V＋...（主要子句）only if（＝ as long as，只要……）S+V... 。

否定：Unless（＝ If... not）＋S＋V...（若非……）；S＋V＋...
（主要子句）。

（3） 表示讓步的副詞子句：

① 雖然 S+V... , 但是 S + V...

Though （＝Although） S + V... , S + V...

=（形容詞、副詞、名詞）+ as + S + V... , S + V...

② 縱使+ S+ V... , S+V...

Even if （＝ Even though） +S +V, S+V...

③ 無論怎樣（困難）……，S+V...

No matter how （＝ However） （difficult）it may be, S+V...

④ 儘管（他）如何（貧窮），他卻相當誠實。

In spite of （=Despite, With all, For all） his poverty, he is very
honest.

⑤ A 之於 B，猶如 C 之於 D

As （C）is to （D）, so is （A） to （B）.

=（A） is to （B） what （C） is to （D）.

（4） 表示比較的副詞子句：

① than 用於比較級

② as... as：如同……一樣

③ The＋比較級……，the＋比較級……：愈……，愈……

The sooner... , the better... ,

例如：AA值愈大，BB結果愈佳

The larger the AA value （is） , the better the BB result becomes.

（不夠簡潔，應修改成下式較佳）

A larger AA implies a better BB result.

（5） 表示時間與地方的副詞子句：When + S + V... = On + Ving 當……之時，例如：我一收到評審者的回音就會馬上通知你。

I will inform you on receiving （=when I receive） any response from reviewers.

20. 非限定有連接詞無動詞子句：「if possible」、「if available」、「if permitted」、「if given the opportunity」、「Before leaving」、「when deciding up... 」、「although accepting... 」例如：他雖然承認復甦跡象微弱，他還是把復甦前景描述為「不可能」He described that prospect as "unlikely", although accepting that any signs of recovery were weak.

若可能，我想要將命名爲「A」，我的論文刊登在……期刊上

I would like my paper entitled "A" to be published in Journal of... if possible.

21. 一個段落以單一相關主旨（中心觀念）爲原則避免超過兩個：以主題句爲段落開頭，然後說明與加強此主題。

例如：Topic sentences often occur at the beginning of a paragraph, followed by material that develops, illustrates, or supports the main point.

22. 下列動詞之後若緊接著動詞當受詞改成動名詞，即動詞＋V-ing

例如：admit、anticipate、appreciate、avoid、complete、consider、delay、deny、discuss、dislike、enjoy、finish、keep、mention、mind、miss、postpone、practice、quit、recall、recollect、resent、resist、risk、suggest、tolerate、understand

23. 在構思每一句子時，不要把主要中心思想放置在句中央，而應放置在句首或句尾爲佳。一般口語化句子，常常會把句子中心思想點擺在句子開始，然後再說明理由與立論點，此種句子稱爲鬆散句（loose sentence）；另外有一種句子是先說明理由與立論點最後再點出中心思想點，稱爲 periodic sentence 雖然後者較具說服力但易淪爲說教，偶而採用就好了。

例如：Considering the free health care, the low crime rate and the comprensive social programs, I am willing to pay slightly higher taxes for the privilege of living in Canada. (Periodic sentence)

I am willing to pay slightly higher taxes for the privilege of living in Canada, considering the free health care, the low crime rate and the comprensive social programs. (Loose sentence)

24. 科技英文常見「As＋動詞過去分詞+……，」的分詞構句句型是屬於省略「主詞＋Be動詞」的形容詞子句修飾主要子句之主詞。常見如下：

（1） as shown in Fig. 1，如圖1所示。

The form drag of a moving object increases as the square of velocity, as shown in Fig. 1.

（2） as already explained,... = as already stated,... ，正如已說明過的。

As already explained, the experimental error is still as small as two percent.

（3） as mentioned above = as pointed out above = as already referred to 正如上述所提到的。

The result at which parameter X reaches a critical value shows an optimum value, as mentioned above.

（4） as previously stated，正如已前說明的。

As previously stated, radiation is the process by which energy is transmitted through space in the absence of matter.

（5） as indicated in... , = as demonstrated in... ，正如在……所顯示的。

The data of parameter Y show a significant increase in decreasing X, as indicated in Table 2.

（6） As widely recognized，正如廣泛所認同的。

As widely recognized, gas expands more rapidly than solid does when heated.

25. 科技英文常見 插入句的句型「as +（名詞+）（助動詞）+動詞……」屬於形容詞子句當作主要子句限定用語。常見如下：

（1） as is known to us, ，正如吾人所知那樣。

As is known to us, the sun rises in the east.

（2） as we know, ，正如吾人所知那樣。

Metals, as we know, conduct heat more rapidly than non-metals do.

（3） as often happens, ，正如經常發生那樣。

He is, as often happens, late for work.

（4） as the name indicates, ，顧名思義。

As the name indicates, a semiconductor owns poorer conductivity than a conductor, but better conductivity than an insulator.

（5） as will be pointed out later,，正如後面指出那樣。

Radiant, electrical, and chemical energies can, as will be pointed out later, all be converted into heat.

26. 科技英文常見「關係連接詞（if、though、while、when、whenever、wherever、whether、however）＋主詞＋Be＋形容詞（或名詞）」經常省略其中 主詞＋Be，尤其當主詞與主要子句相同時。常見如下：

（1） If free from external forces, an object will move with constant velocity.（省略 an object is）

（2） The manuscript entitled on "..." is considered for publication in the Journal of ~ if possible.（省略 it is）

（3） This medicine is good for your health though bitter.（省略 it is）

（4） This chicken soup tastes great while hot.（省略 it is）

（5） The copper is comparatively cheap and has a very good conductivity. Hence, the copper is widely used in electronics cooling wherever possible.（省略 it is）

（6） John tried to work out his project, however difficult.（省略 the project is）

（7） All matter, whether large or small, is made up of molecules.（省略 it is）

27. 獨立分詞片語中主詞與主要子句中的主詞不同時，獨立分詞片語不可
將獨立分詞片語中的主詞省略。

（1） Time permitting; we will pay you a visit next week.

（2） The class being over; the students rushed out of the classroom.

28. 分詞片語中主詞與主要子句中主詞相同時，經常省略主詞與Be。

（1） （Being） a graduate student, you need to improve your technical
writing.

（2） I will attend this conference, if invited.

（3） I usually enjoy listening music （while） driving my car.

☆ 讀者心得增補筆記欄 ☆

二、 科技英文寫作常見文法錯誤與更正匯集

1. 注意科技論文在結論的動詞時態通常使用現在完成式；在引言若講本論文則用現在式；若提別人研究則用過去式。

   （1） Conclusion. This report presented a design of a temperature measurement circuit for the microprocessor.（誤）

   （2） Conclusion. This report has presented a design of a temperature measurement circuit for the microprocessor.

   （3） Introduction. John's report [1995] has presented a design of a temperature measurement circuit for the microprocessor.（誤）

   （4） Introduction. John's report [1995] presented a design of a temperature measurement circuit for the microprocessor.

2. 擺錯修飾語的位置。

   （1） My family almost ate all of the Thanksgiving turkey.（誤）

   （2） My family ate almost all of the Thanksgiving turkey.

   （3） After our conversation lessons, we could understand the English spoken by our visitors from London easily.（誤）

   （4） We could easily understand the English spoken by our visitors from London.

3. 擺錯片語或子句型修飾語的位置

（1）By accident, he poked the pretty girl with his finger in the eye.（誤）

（2）By accident, he poked the pretty girl in the eye with his finger.

（3）I heard that my roommate intended to hold a surprise party for me while I was outside her bedroom window.（誤）

（4）While I was outside her bedroom window, I heard that my roommate intended to hold a surprise party for me.

（5）I heard that she got married to a count with a vast fortune in a small church in Italy.（誤）

（6）I heard that she got married in a small church in Italy to a count with a vast fortune.

4. 擺錯修飾語主詞，修飾語所指的主詞與主要子句主詞不同是不對的

（1）To calculate the strain, ε, the following equation is used:

$$\varepsilon = \frac{\sigma}{E}, \qquad (1)$$

where σ is the normal stress and E is the modulus of elasticity.（誤）

（2）To calculate the strain, ε, we used the following equation:

$$\varepsilon = \frac{\sigma}{E}, \qquad (1)$$

where σ is the normal stress and E is the modulus of elasticity.

（3）To achieve the good quality of studying, the effects of the noise factors must be minimized.（誤）

（4）To achieve the good quality of studying, one must minimize the effects of the noise factors.

5. 不平行對稱的錯誤。

（1）Jenny selected physics, mathematics, and joined the student association.（誤）

（2）Jenny selected physics and mathematics, and joined the student association.

（3）This report is an overview of the processes involved, the problems encountered, and how they were rectified.（誤）

（4）This report is an overview of the processes involved, the problems encountered, and the solutions devised.

（5）I saw where my mistakes lay and how to make up for them.（誤）

（6）I saw where my mistakes lay and how I could make up for them.

6. 擺錯修飾語主詞，修飾語所指的主詞與主要子句主詞不同是不對的。

（1）In contacting the faculty of NTU, John is known to be the smartest student in his class.（誤）

（2）From the faculty of NTU, we learned that John is the smartest student in his class.

（3）Raised in Green Island, it is natural to miss the smell of the sea.（誤）

（4）Raised in Green Island, I often miss the smell of the sea.

（5）For a person raised in Green Island, it is natural to miss the smell of the sea.

（6）Based on the results, we concluded that...（誤）

（7）From the results, we concluded that...

（8）The present results concluded that...

7. however 與 therefore 之前若無「；」，則不能連接兩個獨立句子。

（1）John is a smart student, however, he is lazy.（誤）

（2）John is a smart student; however, he is lazy.

（3）John is a smart student, but is lazy.（誤）

（4）John is a smart student, but he is lazy.

（5）John is a smart student. John, however, is lazy.

（6）The experiment had been left unobserved for too long, therefore it failed.（誤）

（7）The experiment had been left unobserved for too long; therefore it failed.

8. 代名詞「It」不清楚。「this」或「that」（不能單獨以主詞出現），

除非其後緊跟著名詞且該名詞在前一個句子出現過。

（1）Because the instructor assigned a tough project in his class, it gave the

student lot of pressure.（誤）（it may be project or class）

（2）Because the instructor assigned a tough project in his class, this project

gave the student lot of pressure.

（3）The group wanted to meet in March, but this didn't happen until May.

（誤）

（4）The group wanted to meet in March, but the conference didn't take

place until May.

（5）In the report it suggests that moderate exercise is better than no

exercise at all.（誤）

（6）The report suggests that moderate exercise is better than no exercise at

all.

9. 副詞子句省略的主詞與主要子句主詞不同是不對的。

（1）Used properly, you will have a fine paper from your software package.

（誤）（One might ask how "properly" is to be used.）

（2）If you use a software package properly, you will produce a fine paper.

◎ 注意：副詞子句功用如同句子副詞修飾動詞、形容詞、副詞。

They may tell how, why, when, where, etc. Conjunctions used include although, after, if, because, while, since, whether.

10. 副詞子句省略的主詞與主要子句主詞不同是不對的。

（1）Marching in formation, the President reviewed the troops.（誤）

又不是總統在整隊行進？

（2）The President reviewed the troops as they marched in formation.

（3）Born in New Zealand, it is natural to enjoy eating roast lamb.（誤）

（4）For a person born in New Zealand, it is natural to enjoy eating roast lamb.

11. 對等子句若主詞不同，省略其一主詞是不對的。

（1）The computer printouts are ready to be taken to the energy lab and please deliver them promptly.（誤）

（2）The computer printouts are ready to be taken to the energy lab. Please deliver them promptly.

（3）By manipulating the lower back, the pain was greatly eased.（誤）

（4）By manipulating the lower back, the therapist greatly eased the pain.

12. 副詞子句省略的主詞與主要子句主詞不同是不對的；主動語態較佳。

（1）The design was rendered in blue and green and had lines forming the boundary and there were circles added to the perimeter to give it interest.（誤）

（2）The design was rendered in blue and green, with lines forming the boundary and with circles added to the perimeter for interest.

（3）When not going to college, my hobbies range from athletics to automobiles. （誤）

（4）When I am not going to college, my hobbies range from athletics to automobiles.

（5）Before submitting a graduate school application, the university should be selected. （誤）

（6）A student should select the university before submitting a graduate school application.

（7）While analyzing the samples, the error was detected by the technician. （誤）

（8）The technician detected the error while analyzing the samples.

（9）After bleeding the mice, radio-immunoassays were conducted to test binding capabilities. （誤）

（10）After we bled the mice, we conducted radio-immunoassays to test binding capabilities.

13. 副詞子句省略的主詞與主要子句主詞不同是不對的。

（1）Filled with bad gas, he drove his car to Taipei despite the knocking. （誤）

（2）Although it was filled with bad gas, he drove his car to Taipei despite the knocking.

（3）Using a filter on a computer monitor, the radiation can be reduced by more than 90%.（誤）

（4）Using a filter on a computer monitor, one can reduce the radiation by more than 90%.

（5）Although nearly finished, we left the play early because we were worried about our sick dog.（誤）

（6）Although the play was nearly finished, we left early because we were worried about our sick dog.

（7）Comparing with Kaohsiung, the living standard in Taipei is very high. （誤）

（8）Compared with that in Kaohsiung, the living standard in Taipei is very high.（除了被動，仍須注意兩者比較時採對稱結構）

14. 未使用平行對稱結構。

（1）I was glad to be departing for Poland but I was nervous when I left my apartment.（誤）

（2）I was glad to be departing for Poland but nervous to leaving my apartment.

（3）The earthquake not only wrecked railway lines but also the trains.（誤）

（4）The earthquake wrecked not only railway lines but also the trains.

（5）The patient felt much better in the morning than afternoon.（誤）

（6）The patient felt much better in the morning than in the afternoon.

15. 未使用平行對稱結構。

（1）This system excels at tasks such as communicating with other computers, processing records, and mathematical calculation.（誤）

（2）This system excels at tasks such as communicating with other computers, processing records, and calculating mathematical equations.

（3）Eating huge meals, snacking between meals, and too little exercise can lead to obesity.（誤）

（4）Eating huge meals, snacking between meals, and exercising too little can lead to obesity.

16. 不要以介系詞結尾。

（1）All of these rules and regulations should be made aware of.（誤）

（2）Athletes should be made aware of all these rules and regulations.

17. 語態錯誤；一個句子不要超過兩個觀念。

（1）Home care has been expanding tremendously over the past few years partly due to recent technological advances.（誤）

（2）Home care has expanded tremendously over the past few years. This increase is partly due to recent technological advances.

18. 儘量使用主動語態，尤其以人物當主詞勝過以觀念當主詞。

（1）It is through this essay that the proposed benefits of active exercise for Chronic Lower Back Pain （CLBP） will be examined.（誤）

（2）This essay will examine the proposed benefits of active exercise for Chronic Lower Back Pain （CLBP）.

19. 兩個對等子句使用 and、or、nor、but、so、yet、for 連接時，其前需用「，」或者直接用「；」分開

（1）Power corrupts and absolute power corrupts absolutely.（誤）

（2）Power corrupts, and absolute power corrupts absolutely.

（3）Power corrupts; absolute power corrupts absolutely.

20. 採用「，」在一系列中每項之後。

（1）Many studies indicate favorable results in function, decreased pain and range of motion.（誤）

（2）Many studies indicate favorable results in function, decreased pain, and range of motion.

21. 注意片語諸如「as well as」、「in addition to」和「along with」並不與「and」相同，前三者動詞時式與第一主詞一致。

（1）The rose, as well as the tomatoes, are red.（誤）

（2）The rose, as well as the tomatoes, is red.

22. 避免在句子開始使用「this」或「that」（不能單獨以主詞出現），除非其後緊跟著名詞且該名詞在前一個句子出現過。

Avoid starting a sentence with the pronoun "this" or "that" unless it is followed by a noun or refers clearly and directly to a noun in the previous sentence.

（1）A scientist's work has no value unless he shares his thoughts with the scientific community. That is the cornerstone of science.（誤）

（2）A scientist's work has no value unless he shares his thoughts with the scientific community. That communication is the cornerstone of science.

23. 避免在句子開始使用「there is」或「there are」。

（1）After you complete these programs, there are many leagues available for you to join.（不佳）

（2）After you complete these programs, many leagues are available for you to join.

（3）After you complete these programs, you can join one of the many leagues available.

24. 儘量簡潔不要太冗長

（1）It is expected by management that great progress will be made by personnel in providing a solution to these problems in the near future.

（冗長且使用被動語態）

（2）Management expects that personnel will soon solve these problems.

25. 不要在一個句子，甚至一個段落開始使用「And」、「Or」、「So」等。也不要在句子開始使用「I」或「We」避免主觀意識之表達，例如：「I believe」、「We feel」。

不過，若「We」代表作者與讀者是可接受的，例如：In the present paper, we investigate that... 或 We conclude that... 但少用為宜。

26. 錯將不定詞 to 與 V 分開

（1）The marketing group voted to, before they launched the new software, run an anticipatory ad campaign.（誤）

（2）The marketing group voted to run an anticipatory ad campaign before they launched the new software.

（3）The surgeon was able to quickly and painlessly remove the stitches from Greta's forehead.（誤）

（4）The surgeon was able to remove the stitches quickly and painlessly from Greta's forehead.

（5）To better understand the differential equation, I start to study calculus.（誤）

（6）To understand the differential equation better, I start to study calculus.

27. 注意比較或類比時常遺漏些指示代名詞如that；有時遺漏前述介係詞。

（1）The measure was more valid than Smith et al.（1994）（誤）

（2）The measure was more valid than that of Smith et al.（1994）

（3）The method was similar to an earlier study.（誤）

（4）The method was similar to that of an earlier study.

（5）We experienced fewer problems with the revised instrument than the published version.（誤）

（6）We experienced fewer problems with the revised instrument than with the published version.

28. 注意 owing to 前面的逗點「，」不可遺漏；due to 則不要逗點。

（1）The data was lost owing to computer malfunction.（誤）

（2）The data were lost, owing to computer malfunction.

（3）The loss of data was due to computer malfunction.

29. 注意 owing to 是副詞片語，不能當補語或形容名詞；due to 是形容詞

片語，不能修飾動詞或形容詞。

（1）We did not go for picnic due to raining.（誤）（due不能修飾go）

（2）The missing of our picnic is due to raining.（當主詞補語）

（3）We did not go for picnic because of raining.

（4）We did not go for picnic, owing to raining.

（5）There was an increase in the man's temper owing to the poor English.

（誤）

（6）There was an increase in the man's temper due to the poor English.（修

飾名詞increase）

30. 中國學生常寫錯的句子：「造成甚麼結果的理由是因為……」。

（1）The reason for... is due to that.（誤）

（2）The reason for... is that...

（3）The reason for... is that the...

31. 注意 which 不能代表前面句子；of which 係關係詞所有格。

（1）Both bombs produce the same three effects: heat, blast, and radiation. The first of which usually causes the most fatalities.（誤）

（2）Both bombs produce the same three effects: heat, blast, and radiation. The first of these three usually causes the most fatalities.

（3）Heat, blast, and radiation are the bomb's three main effects, the first of which usually causes the most fatalities.

32. therefore （= thus） 與otherwise之前若無「；」，則不能連接兩個獨立句子。

（1）John studies hard everyday, therefore（=thus）, he has very good academic record.（誤）

（2）John studies hard everyday. Therefore（=Thus）, he has very good academic record.

（3）John studies hard everyday; therefore, he has very good academic record.

（4）An oval shape is necessary in the die cavity, otherwise, the flow of metal from the hammering would be restricted.（誤）

（5）An oval shape is necessary in the die cavity; otherwise, the flow of metal from the hammering would be restricted.

33. 注意 like 只接名詞片語，不像 as 可接子句。

（1）Using geothermal energy does not pollute the environment like the burning of fossil fuels does.（誤）

（2）Using geothermal energy does not pollute the environment as the burning of fossil fuels does.

34. 注意 over 與 more than 的區別；over 係指位置，而 more than 係指數量。

（1）The truss had spans of 210 feet and was over 20 feet deep.（誤）

（2）The truss had spans of 210 feet and was more than 20 feet deep.

35. 注意 compare to（當作不相同之比喻）與 compare with（當作同種類比較的區別）。

（1）One may compare three automobiles with each on the criteria of performance, cost, and safety, but John compared water and fish to grass and horse.

（2）One may conclude that the music of Brahms compares to that of Beethoven, but to do that, one must first compare the music of Brahms with that of Beethoven.

（3）Compared to molten salt, liquid sodium is a much more dangerous heat transfer fluid.（誤）

（4）Compared with molten salt, liquid sodium is a much more dangerous heat transfer fluid.

36. 注意 the 定冠詞的用法：遇到不可數之指定名詞需使用定冠詞。

（1）I dove into water.（誤）

（2）I dove into the water.

（3）I saw milk spill.（誤）

（4）I saw the milk spill.

37. 注意 cite（動詞）上網與 site 網站（名詞）的區別。

（1）When you site something from the Internet, you need to include the cite of the address.（誤）

（2）When you cite something from the Internet, you need to include the site of the address.

38. 注意有無逗點。

（1）Jenny studies hard, and thus has a good GPA.（誤）

（2）Jenny studies hard and thus has a good GPA.

（3）Jenny studies hard and she thus has a good GPA.（誤）

（4）Jenny studies hard, and she thus has a good GPA.

39. 科技論文重視客觀。因此，第一人稱「I」或「We」應避免使用。

（1）I believe there is a large potential for...（不佳）

（2）This paper assumes that there is a large potential for...

（3）A common view is that there is a large potential for...

（4）One hypothesis is that there is large potential for...

（5）We found that the first procedure did not work.（不佳）

（6）This paper indicated that the first procedure did not work.

40. 注意 bring 與 take 的區別。

（1）When we go to the party on Saturday, let's bring a bottle of wine.

   （誤）

（2）When we go to the party on Saturday, let's take a bottle of wine.

（3）When you go to the party on Saturday, please bring a bottle of wine.

41. 注意 healthful（有益身體健康的）與healthy（健康的）的區別。

（1）Swimming is a healthy sport.（誤）

（2）Swimming is a healthful sport.

（3）Although he is very old, he is still healthful.（誤）

（4）Although he is very old, he is still healthy.

42. 注意 thus （如此一來）與therefore（因此）的區別。

（1）I am a citizen of Kaohsiung. Thus, I am a Taiwanese.（誤）

（2）I am a citizen of Kaohsiung. Therefore, I am a Taiwanese.

43. 注意動詞的單複數

（1）A variety of issues were presented at the conference.（誤）

（2）A variety of issues was presented at the conference.

44. 注意副詞子句中的主詞，若與主要子句主詞不同時，不可省略副詞子句中主詞或be動詞。

（1）When varying the values of parameter A, the analytical result shows in good agreement with the experimental one.（誤）

（2）When one varies the values of parameter A, the analytical result shows in good agreement with the experimental result

（3）Before submitting for application of graduate study, the graduate school should be selected.（誤）

（4）Before one submits for application of graduate study, the graduate school should be selected.

☆ 讀者心得增補筆記欄 ☆

貳

書面報告篇

一、論文標題 (Title)

好的標題是以最少的文字即可適當表現論文內容爲原則。標題主要包括研究的主題；研究的類型或方法；研究的範圍與目的。 通常標題是由不含動詞的名詞構句所組成，不一定要是完整句子；但是以完整句子爲標題時，必須文法正確。東方學者喜歡「與……有關的調查或研究」，例如：「An Investigation on... 」、「A Study of (on)... 」、「A Research of... 」爲題目，並不是很好的標題，論文研究可省略調查或研究等字眼，仍不言自明。至少歐美學者較少用；好效果的標題通常是以「主題」與「目的」爲命名。另外，應避免縮寫性文字或深奧（艱澀）的文字。像創新 (novel) 等字也不要使用。因每篇論文都或多或少創新觀念或方法。

1. 以「主題」（Subject) 爲命名的範例：通常以研究屬性 (Subject of research field) 爲標題，例如：

……的熱傳分析：Heat Transfer Analysis of...

……的應力分析：Stress Analysis of...

……的自由振動分析：Free Vibration Analysis of...

在……黏彈流體分析：Analysis of a Viscoelastic Fluid in...

在……的太陽能應用：Application of Solar Energy in...

燃料工程之基本模式：Fundamental Models for Fuel Cell Engineering

時間管理之新見解：New light on time management.

近代物理概論：Introduction to modern physics.

2. 以研究類型或方法爲命名的範例：

……的理論分析：Theoretical analysis of...

一簡單解析法求……：A Simple Analytical Method for...

……的數值研究：Numerical Study of...

……的實用方法：A practical approach to...

……的實驗改良：Experimental Improvements of...

A與B的比較：A comparison of A with B.

採用X分析來測定Y：Determination of Y using X analysis

（＝by X analysis）.

3. 以研究內涵與目的爲命名的範例：

X對 Y之影響：Effect（＝Influence）of X on Y.

在……最近的改良：Recent Improvements in...

……的性能最佳化：Performance Optimization of...

……的簡化模式：Simplified Model of...

……的特性預測：Prediction of... Characteristics...

……的最佳運動設計：Optimal Kinematical Design of...

……的現狀與未來趨勢：Present Status and Future Trends of...

☆ 讀者心得增補筆記欄 ☆

二、摘要 (Abstract)

　　論文摘要係將該研究的內容即主題，簡明扼要地陳述出來，並說明本研究的目的，本研究方法，本研究重要結果與發現，最後再與前人比較結果或理論與實驗比較的具體吻合度做總結。總之大致可分成三大部分：

第一：主題句：標明主題與研究目的。

第二：主題後之展開句。

第三：總結（具體成果之闡述與比較）

　　另外，必須注意，在摘要中避免出現：（1）參考文獻與圖表；（2）方程式與數學符號；（3）在本文（In this paper, or In this study）等不必要字眼；（4）致謝詞；（5）第一人稱比較主觀少用，儘量使用第三人稱，亦即「This study；This article；This work；This paper」，而且以主動語態較簡潔有效。

（一）論文主題與研究目的

　　經常擺在論文摘要的第一個句子，又稱主題句（Topic Sentence），注意這一部分的動詞時態，大致使用現在式，可參考如下「套裝句型」：

1. 本論文（或計畫）的目的是（或嘗試）進行研究（或調查）……（主題）。

$$\text{This} \begin{Bmatrix} \textit{paper} \\ \textit{work} \\ \textit{project} \end{Bmatrix} \textbf{ aims to (or attempts to) } \begin{Bmatrix} \textit{study} \\ \textit{investigate} \\ \textit{exa}\text{ mine} \end{Bmatrix} \text{~~~(subject)}$$

$$\text{The} \begin{Bmatrix} \textit{purpose} \\ \textit{aim} \\ \textit{objective} \\ \textit{goal} \end{Bmatrix} \textbf{ of this } \begin{Bmatrix} \textit{paper} \\ \textit{work} \\ \textit{project} \end{Bmatrix} \textbf{ is to } \begin{Bmatrix} \textit{study} \\ \textit{investigate} \\ \textit{exa}\text{ mine} \end{Bmatrix} \text{~~~(subject)}$$

（1） 注意以上兩句型，以第一個較簡潔有效；不過第二個也蠻多人採用。

（2） aim to + V = aim at + Ving

（3） 其他類似：

① 探討……數學模型：to deal with the mathematical model in...

② 建立在……（A）的方法：to develop the method in... (A)

③ 分析……（主題）：to analyze...

④ 了解……的過程：to understand the processes of...

⑤ 提供……方面的量測：to present some measurements of...

⑥ 提供（A）的最佳化，根據（B）理論：to provide optimization of (A) based on (B) theory。

⑦ 著重 Y 對 X 的效應：to focus on effect of Y on X

2. 本研究的焦點在（A主題）。

The study focuses on Topic A.（主動簡潔有效）

= Attention is focused on the study of (A). （也佳較含蓄）

= This study stresses Topic A.

= This study directs our attention to Topic A.

3. 本論文分析（A）並加入考慮（B）效應。

The present study analyzes (A) and takes into account the (B) effects.

4. 本文係發表與討論關於（A）主題的實驗結果。

Experimental results relating to (A) are presented and discussed.

5. 本文係執行一系列實驗以探討（或研究）（A）的效應。

The study conducts a series of experiments on the effects of (A)

= A series of experiments is conducted to study the effects of (A) （較含蓄）

6. 本研究採用 C 的方法探討有關（B）的主題（A）。

This study investigated (A) associated with (B) by using C .

= (A) associated with (B) is investigated using C method. （較含蓄）

7. 採用簡化的模式探討（A）的效應。

A simplified model considers the effect of (A) .

=The effect of (A) is considered using a simplified model.

8. 本論文呈現關於（A）主題的解析研究。

An analytical study on (A) is performed. （較含蓄）

= This paper performs an analytical study on AA.

= This paper studies analytically on AA.（較強有效）

9. 本文建立一套簡單通用方法來預測在平板、圓柱與圓球等形狀物體上的……。

A simple general method is developed to predict... from body shapes such as flat plates, circular cylinders, and spheres. (for a wide range of both Reynolds number and Prandtl number.）

= The developed simple general methods may predict... from body shapes such as flat plates, circular cylinders, and spheres.

10. 本文採用（A）觀念並且引入（B）參數進行分析。

This analysis uses the (A) concept and introduces parameter of B.（主動有效）

=This analysis is performed using the (A) concept and introducing parameterof B.

11. 本研究調查（...A）如何影響（...B）在（...C）上。

This study examines (or investigates）how (... A) affects (... B) in (... C) .

12. 本分析（執行）研究（...A）。

An analysis is carried out (or conducted) to study (... A) .

= The analysis studies (... A) .

13. 本文發表一創新方法以研究（... A）的流動特性。

    A novel method to study the flow characteristics of (... A) is presented.

    =A novel method presents the study on the flow characteristics.

14. 主題（... A）在領域（... B）下，加入考慮（... C）效應所作的分析。

    （... A) has been analyzed for (... B) taking into account (... C) effects.

15. 本文採用（... B）方法完成理論研究（... A）。

    A theoretical study of (... A) has been performed using the (... B) method.

    = (... B) method performs a theoretical study on A（主動有效）

16. 本文進行調查（... A）的使用。

    This paper describes an investigation into the use of (... A) .

17. 本實驗研究（執行）調查（... A）的機構。

    An experimental study investigates the mechanism of (... A) .（主動有效）

    = An experimental study is carried out to investigate the mechanism of (... A）．

18. 採用（... B定律）探討（主題... A）。

    （Subject... A) is examined, utilizing (the... B law）．

    =The... B law examines the subject... A.

19. (... A分析）科技根據（... B）理論應用在（... C）的最佳設計。

    (... A analysis) techniques based on the (... B) theory are applied to the optimal design of (... C) .

= Basing on the (... B) theroy, one may apply (... A analysis) technigues to the optimal design of (... C)

20. 加入考慮（... B）與（... C）下，研究（主題... A）。

（Subject... A) is studied taking into account (... B) and (... C) .

= One may study subject (... A) with taking (... B) and (... C) into account.

（二）主題後之展開句

通常在主題句後，開始陳述本研究重點結果與發現。

一般而言，在摘要中介紹本研究的實驗、數值或推導過程時，請用過去式；因這些結果與發現是本文寫作之前做的，故用過去式。但是，若發現內容具有普遍性，類似普遍真理則改用現在式。可參考如下「套裝句型」：

1. 本文結果顯示（……）。

$$\text{The present results} \begin{cases} \textit{showed} \\ \textit{indicated} \\ \textit{demonstratel} \\ \textit{revealed} \end{cases} \text{that (...)}$$

2. 實驗結果顯示如何（……）。

The experimental results demonstrated how (...)

3. 本研究發表使用解析模式的計算結果與（……）的測試，實驗結果比較。

The study compares (= presents a comparison of) the results computed

using an analytical model with the experimental results of the (...) test.

4. 採用（……）的實驗證實了本數學模式的結果。

The results of the mathematical model were verified experimentally using

(...) = (...) verified experimentally the results of the mathematical model.

5. 本文發現（... A）對（... B）具有明顯（相當程度）效應（或影響）。

（... A) was observed to have significant (or strong) effects (or influences)

on (... B) . = This article obserued that (... A) influences (... B) significantly.

6. 文中（... A）對（... B）的效應顯示出（... C）的下降係由於（... D）的減少。

The effect of (... A) on (... B) shows that (... C) is reduced due to decrease in

(... D) .

7. 本研究進行調查或評估……課題（對流熱傳的平均值）。

We conduct an investigation on the subject (the mean value of convection

heat transfer) = This study investigates the topic on... .

（三）摘要結尾總結（具體成果的闡述與比較）

大致以一或兩句作總結，有時與前人結果做比較當總結，通常用現在完成式，例如「最後，本文計算值與實驗比較時達成很好的吻合度。」：

Finally, a good agreement between the calculated and experimental values has been achieved. = Finally, the calculated and experimental values reach (= come to) a good agreement.

不過也可用現在式動詞時態或助動詞表現。可參考如下「套裝句型」：

例如：本研究的下一步將著重於……方面

The next step of the investigation will focus on...

例如：本文簡要地介紹了現有設備及其用法

A brief description of the test equipment available and its application is also included.

例如：這項技術今後將可能運用在飛航零件上

This technology will probably find application in making parts for space flight.

◎強調本論文的重要性與價值，其「套裝句型」參考如下：

1. 本文比較理論與實驗結果，顯示出良好的一致性

   A comparison between the analytical and experimental results shows good agreement.

2. 本文比較理論與實驗結果，顯示出良好的一致性

   A good agreement has been found between the theoretical and experimental results.

3. 從⋯⋯方面，為達到這些需求，本文建議各種不同模式以探討⋯⋯

   A variety of models for Ving has been proposed to meet these needs, from...

4. 本文已討論並提出⋯⋯的一般原理

   General principles for... are discussed, and... are provided.

5. AA必須達到⋯⋯的特定需求是普遍被接受的。

   It is commonly (or generally) accepted that AA should meet the specific needs of...

6. 在⋯⋯時，另一問題浮現

   Another problem arises when...

三、引言或序論（Introduction）

將相關主題前人研究狀況作陳述與調查，並概略敘述本文將要進行的方向與特點，大致的結構為：（1）一般性場白，即建立本文研究主題與涵蓋領域（the setting）：establish a content and help readers understand how the research fits into a wider field of study；（2）已發表的研究（already studied)：more specific statements about the aspects of the problem already studied by other researchers；（3）研究需求即尚未研究的範圍（investigation needed or the area is not treated in the previous literature）：statements that indicate the need for more investigation；（4）本研究之目的（purpose）：very specific statement (s) giving the purpose/ objectives of the writer's study；（5）本研究的價值（即實用性與優點）（value）：optional statement (s) that gives a value or justification for carrying out the study.

（一）一般性開場白

首先說明本文研究領域的背景資料與重要性，從與其相關更廣範圍的研究狀況開始，然後再縮小範圍至本文研究領域。大約一開頭前兩三句或一小段落即可。例如：「凝結熱傳研究」屬於相變化熱傳一種，因此，開場白我會從目前電子冷卻極需要相變化熱傳；或者說電腦CPU之散熱遇

到瓶頸，因此相變化熱傳模式再度吸引許多專家學者注意與研究，再切入凝結熱傳研究之重要性。為了強調本文研究領域之重要性，在此特別就常常出現用語，如「吸引許多專家學者注意與研究」等相關表現。常用參考「套裝句型」：

1. 大量文獻投入（... A）應用領域，已在不少機會（文獻1-3）中被審查過。

   The vast literature devoted to (... A) application has been reviewed on several occasions [1-3].

◎ vast 大量；vast extent 廣大範圍；接單數名詞。

2. 自從（因為）事件後，（... A）主題已成為主要（許多）關心（或用心、注意）的課題。

   Since (Because)... , topic on (... A) has become a matter of great concern.

   = Since (Because)... , much attention (or effort) has been directed to topic A

   = Since... , much effort has been made on topic A.

3. 由於在……領域的實務重要性，A主題已被廣泛研究中。

   Topic A has been widely (= extensively) studied in view of (= because of; due to) the practical importance in the field of... .

4. 由於實務上的重要性，關於（... A）與（... B）問題理論分析，已被發表過許多篇。

Because of its practical importance (=Both on practical and important grounds) , many theoretical analyses have been made concerning the (... A) and (... B) problems.

5. 自從（因爲）事件（參考文獻）後，大量文獻投入預測（或研究）……

Much work (=literature) has been performed in predicting (or studying)... since the... [Reference].

6. 雖然……已成爲在……領域重要關切課題，不過目前爲止……仍是未甚清楚。

Although... became a great concern in the field of... ,... has not been understood clearly so far. (= it still remains an unsettled question so far.)

7. 最近……研究急速發展，其成果受到很大的注意。

Recently the study of... have developed rapidly and its achievements have become a center of attraction.

◎ 注意有些名詞必須使用單數如：literature、information、interest（興趣）。

1. 習慣單數形：much (or little) effort、much (or little) interest、much (or little) attention、much (or little) research、much (or little) work。

2. 亦有習慣複數形：many (or few) attempts、many (or few) investigations、many (or few) studies、many (or few) researchers。

其他常用參考「套裝句型」：

1. 吸引許多人在……的興趣

   attract much interest in...

2. 吸引更進一步探討……

   receive further consideration in...

3. 視為目前研究重要特性

   be recognized as a characteristic feature of current research.

4. 許多……研究目前積極在進行中

   Much active research on... is current in progress.

5. 積極進行研究……

   make (=carry out, conduct) active research into...

6. 集中注意在……研究

   focus one's attention on the study of or direct one's attention to the study of...

7. ……在……領域之研究已廣泛被接受與應用

   ... has been widely accepted and applied in the field of...

8. ……相當被看重

   ... is considered of great importance.

9. ……在全世界上，正快速發展中

   ... is being rapidly developed over the world.

10. ……是不可忽視的主題

... is a topic that one should not ignore.

11. 變成重要的（實際的）問題在處理……上

to become important（practical）problems on dealing with...（=handling of... ）

（二）已發表的研究

寫前人研究狀況作陳述與調查時，可依：（1）與主題相關的發表時間先後陳述；（2）與主題接近相關性程度而進行；（3）依研究方法作調查陳述。

首先針對與主題相關的發表時間先後陳述，如何使用好的連接詞是相當重要，茲示範如下：

1. 首先，AA主張……：Firstly, AA advocated that...

2. 然後，BB進一步發表……：Then, BB further presented that...

3. 之後，CC也探討……：Afterwards, CC also investigated that...

4. 最近，DD研究……：More recently, DD studied that...

再者，若同時敘述兩種不同觀點，要把它們分開，茲示範如下：

1. AA首先提出：AA firstly put forward that...

2. 相反，BB相信……：In contrast, BB believed...

或者，不像AA，BB提議……：Unlike AA, BB suggest...

若同時敘述兩種接近觀點，要把它們分開，茲示範如下：

1. AA 建議……：AA suggest that...

2. 相似地（對等之下），BB也陳述……：Similarly, (Alternatively)，BB also showed that...

其次要注意提及前人研究的動詞時態：

1. 若是屬於報告眞理與事實（reporting facts），請使用現在式：

Topic+ verb (present) + fact + (Reference)

例如： 在牛頓著作 [1] 陳述兩物體間存在萬有引力。

There exists a universal gravitational force between two bodies in Newton [1].

2. 若一次提到許多作者在此一主題發表過研究時，請使用現在完成式，茲示範如下：

（1） Authors+ verb (present perfect) + Topic+ (References) 常用參考「套裝句型」：

例如：數個研究者〔Rose 1990; Yang 1998; Jacobi 1999〕探討過……

（主題）

Several researchers have studied... (topic) [Rose 1990; Yang 1998;

Jacobi 1999]

最近，由 [Refs...] 完成數個實驗顯示，在什麼情況下，……過程

為……

More recently, several experiments performed by [Refs...] have

shown that in the case of... , the process of... is...

（2） Topic + verb (present perfect) + Author + (References) 常用參考「套

裝句型」：

① 數個文件 (Rose 1995, and Jacobi 1999) 顯示（證實）……

Several articles [Rose 1995, and Jacobi 1999] have shown (con-

firmed) that...

② 數個研究者 [Rose 1990; and Yang 1998] 探討過……的強化

The enhancement of... has been studied by several investigators

[Rose 1990, and Yang 1998].

3. 在未特定指明那些文獻下，提到目前或多或少已發表過相關主題研究

時，請使用現在完成式。研究多寡＋動詞（現在完成式）＋主題；常

用參考「套裝句型」：

（1）大量文獻探討過……（主題）

Vast literature has been investigated on (... the topic) .

（2）僅少數嘗試在……上作研究

Only few attempts (or studies) have been made at...

= The literature, however, is limited on the study of...

4. 若提及特定作者的結果發現與使用方法時，請使用過去式：

作者 (Reference) ＋動詞（過去式）＋that ＋結果發現常用參考「套裝句型」：

（1）Young [1995] 文獻發現（注意；觀察）到（……）。

Young [1995] found (discovered；showed; noted; reported; observed) that...

（2）當Young [1995] 尖銳地指出（提及）……（某事）時。

As Young [1995] acutely referred to the fact that...

= As Young [1995] acutely pointed out that...

（3）早在……世紀，……（某人）就注意到……（某事）。

As early as the... Century, [Ref.] noted (= noticed) that...

（4）大量文獻探討過……（主題），（某文獻）是注意到……（某事）的其中一篇（人）。

Vast literature has been investigated on (... the topic），(...) was among those who noted that...

（5）（某文獻）是第一篇調查（或建立……模式去）。

[Ref.] first investigated (or developed a... model to)...

（6）[Ref.] 以及後來 [Ref.] 實驗證實這個事實。

This fact was confirmed experimentally by [Ref.], and later by [Ref.]

◎　注意，在SCI年度回顧某一主題的期刊論文，只以參考文獻代號
表示其來源時，傾向使用被動語態。

（7）（某文獻）首次系統地進行研究……

The first systematic investigation into... was conducted by [Ref.]

（8）某文獻設計一個近似方法去計算……

[Ref.] worked out an approximate method for the calculation of...

（9）（某文獻）建議使用……當簡單方法來分析……數據。

[Ref.] recommended using... as a simple method for analyzing... data.

（10）（某文獻）發展出一套適合……的近似方法。

[Ref.] developed an approximate method which is suitable in...

（11）[Ref.] 以及[Ref.] 藉由... 的應用，在……問題上執行完整實驗。

[Ref.] and [Ref.] carried out extensive experiments on the problem
of... (Ving) by the application of...

（12）[Ref.] 首度以及後來 [Ref.] 與 [Ref] 借助於……實驗證實……的事
實。

An experimental proof of the fact that... with the aid of... was first
given by [Ref.]; and shortly afterwards by [Ref] and [Ref] .

其他常用參考之過去的研究動作：

1. 理論（或實驗）証實：confirmed theoretically (or experimentally)

2. 提議一個普遍……方法去求解……：proposed a general... method for solving...

3. 使用……科技，推導出……方程式之解：derived a solution of... equation using... technique.

4. 使用……方法來探討……：used a... approach and studied...

5. 提出……理論（觀念）：propounded (presented) a theory (idea) that...

當指出別人研究的缺點或錯誤時，須文詞使用婉轉，不要直接使用負面文字表達「wrong、questionable」描述。參考如下：

1. Their results may be more reasonable if they had considered this situation.

2. Their results could be better convinced if they...

3. Their results may remain some uncertainties.

（三）本研究的需求及尚未研究的範圍

通常需指出，截至目前為止所進行的研究，哪些研究領域仍不甚清楚（因為沒有……）：However, it is unclear about... ,（because there is not... ）

哪些文獻資料是相當欠缺：

1. Little (work, literature, research) has been done (or conducted) on...

2. Few（studies, studies, investigations) have been done (or conducted) on...

或者。極少人注意到（或嘗試在）⋯⋯的研究。

1. Little attention has been focused on...

2. Few attempts have been made to...

3. The literature is limitted on...

或者。以前研究未曾（極少）考慮到哪些點⋯⋯。

Previous research (studies) has (have) + (failed to consider, ignored, neglected to）...

或者⋯⋯領域似乎已成熟建立（或發展），但是哪些因素卻未見發表。

Although... may appear well established in literature, some of... aspects have not been addressed so far.

◎ 注意以上均使用現在完成式被動語態。指出先前的不足，然後可引導出
   研究的需求——新的方法或方向。

   常用參考「套裝句型」：

1. 雖然關於 X 有些現行文獻；不過關於 Y 的資料卻很少。

   Although some literature is available on X, little information is available

   on Y (= little is known about Y = there is little information concerning Y) .

   = Some literature is available on X ; however, the information about Y is

   limitted.

2. 不過，關於目前特定可找到的資料卻很少。

   But, there is little information available on the particular research topic.

3. 雖然許多關於 X 的研究；不過關於目前特定研究主題卻很少。

   While many studies have been done on X, few studies have reported on

   the particular research topic.

4. 遺憾的（令人惋惜的）是，儘管研究的人很多，但在⋯⋯方面卻不多

   It is regretful (= a pity) that, in spite of the large number of researchers,

   only a few studies in... have been done.

5. 雖然許多模式已發展出（研發出），然而⋯⋯的簡單普遍模式仍欠

   缺。

   Although many models have been developed, a simple general model for

   ... is still lacking.

6. 自從⋯⋯，許多文獻已開始注意到⋯⋯；對照之下，關於⋯⋯卻所知

   有限。

   Vast literature has focused on... since... . In contrast, little is known about...

其他常用參考「套裝句型」：

1. 現存許多論文（描述、進行）理論與實驗調查A，但是有關B的研究卻是很少或相差甚遠。

   Many existing papers describe theoretical and experimental investigations into A but studies on B are few and far between.

2. 詳細理論分析 A 已發表在此系列的先前論文[1, 2]。

   Previous papers in this series [1, 2] have reported in detail theoretical analyses on A.

3. 然而有一點尚重要的，就是去了解 A 以 B 的函數關係如何變動。

   It is important though, to understand how A varies a function of B.

4. 某某人 [3] 理論已顯示A受B的影響不明顯。

   Mr. So and So [3] has shown theoretically that A is not significantly affected by B.

5. 改善（A）的性能是藉以增加（B）的重要領域（目標）之一。

   Improving (A) performance is one of the critical areas for increasing (B) .

6. 在（……C）領域關於（……A）的研究並未被廣泛進行。

   The study of (... A) in (... C) has not been fully (or extensively) explored (= conducted or carried out) .

7. 仍有許多未解決的問題，並且……尚未普及。

There are still many problems remaining unsolved and... is not used generally yet.

（四）研究的目的

基於上述的研究需求，我們得以進入簡短陳述本研究的內容與重要創新研究項目或訊息。注意，這裡動詞時態通常使用現在式。常用參考「套裝句型」：

1. 本研究（文）主要目標在探討（發展）……

This study (article, paper or work) aim to investigate (develop)...

= The objective (purpose=goal=aim) of this paper is to investigate...

= The present work is aimed at investigating (developing)...

= Our major aim here is to investigate...

= This article is intended as an investigation of...

= The present paper is written with the aim of developing...

2. 本論文設計（擴展）……的有效方法：

This paper designs (extends) the efficient method of...

3. 本論文報告……：This paper reports on...

4. 本論文提供……結果：This paper provides results of...

5. 我們期望上述疑點（差異），藉著本文建議的方法可解決。

   It is hoped that the above question (discrepancy) will be resolved with

   our proposed method (approach) .

（五）本研究的價值（即實用性與優點）

把本研究的價值突顯出來，如此評審與讀者才有興趣刊出來或看下去。通常強調你是在哪一方面創新。如方法或結果更精確簡潔；或是納入更進一步考慮、應用範圍更廣。均置於引言中的最後一段，即結尾時一兩個句子。常見研究創新。如方法或結果表現範例與常用參考「套裝句型」如下：

1. 本文是第一篇（嘗試）研究（處理）……

   The present study is the first (attempt) to investigate (deal with)...

2. 本研究目的是擴大……的（過程；量測；分析）

   The aim of present study is to extend the (process; measurement; analysis)

   of... for... =The present study aims to extend the process of...

3. 本文獲得好的簡化結果且便於應用

   The present result is useful in its simplicity and easy to apply.

4. 本文所提創的模式可改善應用於……

   The proposed model may prompt application in...

最後，摘錄一些英美學者之「引言」示範：

1. 關於……的問題的理論研究有無數個。

 Theoretical investigations into the problems of... are very numerous.

2. 但是，我們只對提及下列少數作者中較滿意的：[Ref]，[Ref]和[Ref]

 The paper shall be satisfied with the mention of the following few authors

 only: [Ref], [Ref] and [Ref].

3. 尤其把焦點放在此一論文[Ref].

 Particular attention should be given to the paper by [Ref].

4. 此一研究包含……的調查以及描述針對……近似方法來計算……

 This study contains an investigation of... as well as the description of an

 approximate method of calculating... for...

5. 此一方法具有 [Ref] 獲得之實驗結果的優點即顯示……

 The method takes advantage of the (experimental) results due to [Ref]

 which demonstrated that...

四、模式（Modeling）

理工研究論文一般分成理論模式（Theortical Modeling）與實驗模式
（Experimental Modeling）等兩種。

（一）理論模式

理論模式為求建立可解析模式與控制方程式，通常要作一些條例式假設：

1. 假設條件 (Assumption)：注意每一假設條件的英文結構，採同一型態陳述較優美。至於陳述假設條件的方式，可參考如下「套裝句型」：

（1）下列是一系列假設條件用以建立數學模式：（A）……；（B）……

   The following is a list of the assumptions used in developing the mathematical model: (A)... ; (B)...

（2）本文的分析是在如下的主要簡化假定與近似條件進行：

   The main simplifying assumptions and approximations in this analysis are as follows:

（3）本文執行下列假設條件：

   The following assumptions are invoked

   = The assumptions made in this study are the following:

（4）本文所建立模式係採用下列假設：

   The model development is subject to the following (underlying) assumptions:

（5）為求建立本問題方程式，本文作如下假定：

The following assumptions have been made in order to formulate the problem.

= The assumptions for formulating the problem are as follows:

2. 推導公式Formulation：理論分析的研究經常需要數學模式建立與公式的推導，可參考如下「套裝句型」：

（1）加入……作用或計算，我們獲得下列……方程式

Taking into account that... , one may reach at the following... equation:

（2）將 A 和 B 變數導入方程組 (1) 與 (2) 變成兩個……方程式

Variables (... A) and (... B) allow one to transform a system of equations (1) and (2) into two... equations.

（3）方程式 (1) 與 (2) 的起始與邊界條件為……。

The initial and boundary conditions subject to Eqs. (1) and (2) read...

（4）方程組 (1) 與 (2) 配合邊界條件 (3) 與 (4) 的解為……。

The solution of Eqs. (1) and (2) with boundary conditions (3) and (4) reads.

（5）依循我們先前研究所建立的方法，我們在加入考慮 (A) 與 (B) 可獲得下列……方程式。

Following the approach developed in our previous studies (see, eq... .), one may at the following... equation that accounts for (A) and for (B）.

（6）積分 (1) 式並使用起始條件，我們獲得下列關於 (A) 的公式。

Integrating Eq. (1) with the initial condition, one may obtain the following formula for the (A)

（7）將這些假設納入考慮，（主題）A以微分方程式所統御（或表現）。

By taking these assumptions into account, (A) is governed by the differential equation.

（8）經由引入的無因次參數，無因次 (A) 的方程式可寫成為：

By introducing dimensionless parameters, the dimensionless (A) equations can be written as...

（9）(A) 方程式若納入 (B) 效應表成……

The (A) equation, accounting for the (B) effect, is given as...

（10）定義 (A=) 與利用式子 (B)，方程式 (C) 與邊界條件 (D) 可表為……。

Defining (A =...) , and using Eq. (B) , one may write the equation (C) with the boundary condition as...

（11）經由引入下列無因次量……於方程式 (A) 與 (B) 中，能量方程式可變成下式：……與邊界條件……。

By introducing the following dimensionless quantities:... into Eqs. (A) and (B) , the energy equation can be cast into (reduced to) the following form:... with the boundary conditions...

（12）現在使用……乘積於式子 (A) 的兩邊，並用式子 (B) ，吾人終可得（下式）……。

Now applying the... product to both side of Eq. A) and using Eq. (B) , one finally obtains...

（13）在經過演算式子 (A) 積分後，可導出關於AA的下列結果。

After evaluating the integrals in Eq. (A) , one may derive the following results for (AA）.

（14）假設……以及令……為……，我們可寫出……方程式如下式。

Assuming that... , and denoting... by... , one may write... equation of... in the form.

（15）再者，若我們……，我們在……情況下，從……方程式獲得……方程式的修正式。

Further, if one... , one may obtain the following modified form of... equations for the case of... from Eq.

（16）從 (1) 與 (2) 方程式分別代入 X 與 Y，以及從 (3) 與 (4) 方程式代入u 與v，我們可進一步獲得下列關係式。

Substituting, X and Y from Eqs. (1) and (2) , respectively, together with u and v from Eqs. (3) and (4) , one may obtain further the following relation.

（17）在這些假定條件下，在……的……方程式可寫成下式：

Under these assumptions the equation of... in... can be written in the following form:

（18）在……情況下，……方程式簡化成……簡單表示式，以及……分佈方程式因此變爲……。

For the case of... , the... (equation) reduces to the simple expression (... formula) , and the equation for... distribution becomes consequently...

（二）實驗模式

實驗量測的論文必須將「實驗設備與過程」（Experimental Apparatus and Procedure）或者以「材料與方法」（Materials and Methods）等，列出可參考如下「套裝句型」：

1. 本研究所使用的實驗設備有系統地顯示於圖1上。

The experimental apparatus used in the present study is illustrated schematically in Fig. 1.

2. 測試段與熱電偶的位置標示在圖 2 上。

The test section and locations of thermocouples are shown in Fig. 2.

3. 本實驗在（強制對流）條件下進行而實驗參數與範圍顯示於表1上。

The experiments are conducted under (forced convection) condition, and experimental parameters and their ranges are indicated in Table 1.

4. 組成之實驗設備如圖1所示，它包括……。

The experimental set up is shown in Fig. 1. It consists of...

5. 下面進行關於……的實驗：1.……；2.……；3.……。

Following experiments on... were made (or conducted) : 1... , 2... , 3...

☆ 讀者心得增補筆記欄 ☆

五、結果與討論（Results and Discussion）

　　一般論文結果均以圖與表來說明且討論其特色，主要在傳達該篇論文的重要發現，然後與先前已發表著作比較評論，後者屬於討論部分。　因此結果與討論大致分成三部分敘述：

第一、陳述每一張圖片的編號（位置）並以文字說明其結果。

第二、陳述本研究最重要發現與特性。

第三、評論本研究的結果。

　　通常在陳述每一張圖片的位置及說明其結果與重要發現後，隨即評論較為方便對照圖文說明。另外，也有將所有圖位置及說明其結果作完後，再建立另一段討論本研究的結果。

（一）如何評論本研究的結果？其要點包括三點

1. 歸納與推論結果與發現（generalize from the results）：可分類歸納，每一類均由最重要到次重要、由簡入繁方式提出。

2. 闡述造成結果的理由（explain possible reasons for the results）。

3. 與其他已發表著作比較評論（compare the results with those from other studies）。

（二）如何使用正確的動詞時態？

1. 標示圖或表的數據位置時，請用現在式，例如：

（1）……的實驗數據呈現在表1。

The experimental data of... are presented in Table 1.

（2）表2歸納局部熱傳係數的實驗結果。

Table 2 summarizes the experimental results on the local heat transfer coefficient.

2. 陳述圖或表的某一點結果與發現時，為提高說服力，儘量在某一點的結果與發現，提出說明或證據。大部分評審喜歡問你結果與發現的原因在工程與經濟領域的結果與發現，大部分屬於普遍性論點，故常用現在式；其他社會科學領域則使用過去式。評論本研究的結果時：請用現在式；若屬可能推論可使用助動詞，如 may 或 can。

（1）假設不是很肯定研究的結果時，常用參考「套裝句型」：

① ……似乎是……

It appears (seems or is likely) that S +be...

= S+ appear (s) +to be... （此句較簡潔）

② ……AA似乎是造成BB……的原因。

It seems that AA can account for (interpret) BB...

③ 由……結果可陳述爲……。

It may be stated from the... result that...

④ 本結果可歸因於……。

The results may be attributed to... (=due to; caused by)

⑤ (AA）與（BB）之間差異可歸因於……（CC）。

The discrepancy between... (AA) and... (BB) might be caused by... (CC)

（2） 若是比較肯定研究之結果則使用下列「套裝句型」：

① 由圖1清楚顯示……

It is clear (obvious or evident) from Fig. 1 that...

= Fig. 1 clearly (evidently) shows (indicates) that...

② 本研究深信……

The present study assures that...

③ 若結果不是創新的肯定時，通常以「本結果證實……」表示。

The result confirms that...

④ 若結果是肯定創新時，則以「本研究首度發現到……的結果。這個發現將帶給我們……」表示。

The present study discovers (puts forward; observes) that... for the first time. This discovery (=finding; observation) will bring us...

◎ 注意：不可只用 This 取代 This discovery。

3. 與其他已發表著作比較評論時，請用現在式。常用參考「套裝句型」：

（1）「關於（A）的理論結果與（B）的實驗結果吻合度相當良好」

Theoretical results for the (A) agree fairly well with the experimental result of (B) .

（2）「檢視圖1所呈現的結果，顯示實驗結果與理論預測吻合度相當良好」：

Inspection of results presented in Fig.1 shows that the agreement between the experimental results and theoretical prediction is fairly good.

（3）「比較由於摩擦以及壓縮所造成熱導致溫差似乎有用」

It appears useful to compare the temperature differences that result from the heat due to friction with those caused by compression.

（4）由結果進入討論的常用參考「套裝句型」：

① 本結果強調……的重要。

The result emphasizes the importance of...

② 本結果顯示 B 對 C 影響隨 D 與 E 變動

The result indicates that the influence of B on C varies with D as well as with E.

③ 本實驗結果如圖……中曲線（B）所顯示。

The experimental results are indicated in curve B (Fig... .) .

=Curve B in Fig... . demonstrates the experimental results.

④ 由以上獲得結果，接著我們來討論……。

Having the above results, one thus now turns to (discuss)...

⑤ 在完成那一點結果後，下一步我們要……。

Once the result of... point is obtained, the next step is to...

⑥ 知道這些點（……結果），我們可進一步深入……。

With these points (the results of...) in mind, one may look further into...

◎ 注意：With + 名詞 +（介係詞片語；形容詞片語：分詞片語；不定詞片語）意表「伴隨發生……的動作」，例如：當夜晚低垂時，我們啟程賦歸：With night coming on, we started for home.

⑦ 我們可將……觀念擴展到……。

One may expand this idea (result of...) into...

（2）在陳述本研究最重要發現與特性，常使用一些變動與關係的用語如下，常用參考「套裝句型」：

① 在（……）方面，主題傾向增加或減少。

Subject + shows a tendency to increase or decline in (...) (= tended to increase or decline in）...

② ……逐漸加增至最大值（頂點）。

... gradually rises to the maximum value (the peak) .

=... is going up to the peak.

③ ……逐漸下降（減少）至最小值（低點）。

... is gradually reduced to the minimum value (the bottom)

=... falls right down to the bottom.

④ Y 隨 X 兩次方成反比變化。

Y varies as the inverse square of X.

⑤ 研究參數或變數隨（……）變動而增加或減少。

Subject (Variable or parameter) + verb of variation + with (...)

⑥ 如同預測一般，使冷卻速度變慢發現到結晶度與顆粒大小增加。

As expected, the increase in crystallinity and spherulite size is observed with decreasing cooling rate.

（3） 茲歸納表示變動的動詞（Verb of variation）如下：

① 表示「增加」計有：increase、rise、enhance、augment

② 表示「減少」計有：decrease、decline、drop、fall

③ 表示「保持不變（穩定）」：remain constant (steady)

④ 表示「保持上升」：keep rising

例如：「參數 A 隨 B 增加或減少而增加」

Parameter A increases with (increasing or decreasing) B.

（4） 表示變動程度的副詞用語

① 表示「劇烈地；快速地」變動的副詞用語：rapidly、sharply、 dramatically、steeply。

② 表示「明顯地」變動的副詞用語：significantly、greatly、markedly。

③ 表示「輕微地」變動的副詞用語：slightly、negligibly、insignificantly。

④ 表示「驟然地；突然地」變動的副詞用語：abruptly、suddenly。

⑤ 表示「平穩地；逐漸地」變動的副詞用語：steadily, gradually。

（5） 表示變動之名詞片語：

① 輕微增加或減少：a slight increase or decrease

② 快速增加：an immediate sharp increase

③ 大量增加或降低：a large increase or decrease

④ 很清楚地當範圍由小變大時，預測準確度大幅降低。

Clearly, there is a large decrease in predicting accuracy when moving from smaller to larger scales.

⑤ 劇升：a steep rise

驟降：a rapid drop=a sudden dip

⑥ 從……反轉而上：an upturn from...

從……逆轉而下：a downturn from...

（6） 表示關係的程度：

① A 與 B 具有直接關係：A is directly related to B

② A 與 B 具有相當明顯關係：A is significantly (closely or highly) related to B.

（7） 再者，我們將在結果討論時，常用參考「套裝句型」：

① 另外注意由方程式（……）亦指出……」：Also note from Eq. (...) that S+V

② 繼續我們……的討論：continue with our discussion of...

③ 使人深刻理解……的觀念：give one insight into the concept of...

④ 使人信服……的觀念：give credence to the idea that...

⑤ 提供說明……現象：provide explanations for... phenomena

⑥ 使用……定律去解釋……的原因：use the... Law to reason that

⑦ 假定……主張解說此一現象：explain the phenomenon by assuming that...

（8） 討論時常用的表示因果關係的動詞片語（VP）

① 表示造成或導致：cause、lead to、give rise to、result in、contribute to、account for（可解釋成）。

句型：S（原因）＋VP（表示造成或導致）＋O（結果）。

② 表示起因於或歸咎於：result from、arise from、be due to、be attributed to、be caused by

句型：S（結果）＋VP（表示起因於或歸咎於）＋O（原因）。

例如：比較由於摩擦以及壓縮所造成熱導致溫差似乎有用。

It appears useful to compare the temperature differences which result from the heat due to friction with those caused by compression.

例如：Y的增加起因於……X。

The increase in... (Y) results from... (X)

（9） 最後，有關圖之範例，常用參考「套裝句型」：

① 圖1顯示……方程式在不同 P值下的解。

Fig.1 illustrates (= displays) the solutions of... equations for various values of P.

② 在不同參數值 C 值下,（A）係數受（B）的影響呈現在圖1。

The dependences of the (A) coefficients vs. (B) for different values of parameter C are shown in Fig.1.

③ 圖2顯示當 (... A) 參數遞增時，B 係數跟著（輕微）增加。

Fig. 2 demonstrates that as (... A) parameter increases，B coefficient increases (slightly) .

④ 由這些圖可以清楚知道，A 隨 B 與 C 增加而遞增。

From these figures it is clear (or evident) that A increases as B and C increase (or, with increasing B and C .

⑤ （... A）對（... B）關係可由不同參數（C）值畫在圖2上。

In Fig2, (... A) versus (... B) is drawn for several different values of parameter (C) .

⑥ 圖 3 顯示在數種 A 與 B 值下以及當 C=0 與 D=0 情況下，數種溫度分布對應變數關係。

Fig. 3 displays several temperature profiles vs. variable for several values of A and B when C=0 and D=0.

⑦ 由圖3，可以清楚看見 A 隨著具有參數 C 效應的參數 B 增加而遞增。

From Fig. 3, it is evident that (or It is apparent from Fig. 3 that) A increases with an increase in the parameter (B) with the effect of parameter C.

⑧ 圖7顯示當 C 數值分別為 10、20 與 30 下，A 數以 B 參數的函數變化。

Fig.7 presents the variation of (A) number as a function of the (B) parameter for C numbers of 10, 20 and 30.

⑨ 圖 2 與圖 3 包含本文計算 AA 與 BB 的分布與 [Ref3]、[Ref4] 量測值比較。

Figs. 2 and 3 contain a comparison between the calculated AA and BB distribution and those measured by [Ref3] and [Ref4].

⑩ 由圖2，我們可以推斷……。

From Fig. 2, one may deduce that...

⑪ 圖 2 顯示本文在……方面的理論結果與〔Ref〕所執行之量測值比較。

The diagram in Fig. 2 gives a comparison between theoretical results on... with measurements on... performed by [Ref].

六、結論（Conclusion）

一般而言結論的功能可分為三方面，第一、本體資料的總結
（Summary）；第二、本體資料的廣泛解說與推廣範圍（Interpretation and
Limitation）；第三、本體資料的建議與未來研究（Recommendation）。
因此，我們大致可由四個方向來完成結論：

1. 再度確認問題點與主要發現：即再度強調本文之結果與主要發現，但
   注意卻勿直接摘錄前面結果之句子。使用過去式或現在式或完成式動
   詞時態或助動詞＋V 均可，但以現在完成式較佳。常用參考「套裝句
   型」：

   （1）上述的結果可歸納如下：1.……；2.……。

      The foregoing results can be summarized as follows: 1... 2...

   （2）本文主要發現是……, 這個發現是相當實用且重要在設計……

      The main finding of this work is (or was)...

      This finding is of great practical importance for the design of...

   （3）由上述實驗，我們作成下面結論。

      The above experiment concluded that...

   （4）由以上本研究所得結果，我們獲得重要工程結論。

      From the present results obtained, one draw (or drew) the important

      engineering conclusions:

=The present results yield the important engineering conclusion that...

=On the basis (From) the present results obtained, the following

conclusions can (may) be made (drawn, reached)...

（5）基於這些理由，吾人可做如下的結論：

On these grounds, one may come to (draw=reach=arrive at) the

conclusion that...

（6）這些數據證實（導致）如下的結論「……」

These data support (lead to) the conclusion that...

（7）此時吾人可作如下結論……

One may conclude at this point that...

（8）在以上過程，吾人發展解析方法去預測……

The above process developed analytical means for estimating...

2. 本文重要推論的說明：所謂推論，係由某一特定結果推廣至普遍論

點，正好與引言相反。使用現在式動詞時態或助動詞＋V 均可。常用

參考「套裝句型」：

（1）這些結果可能以假定 S＋V 來加以說明

These results can be explained by assuming that S+V...

（2）可能會有如何……的這些結果

It is likely that these results...

（3）由以上結果我們可說……

It may be stated from the above results that...

=One explanation for the above results may be that...

（4）由以上判斷，吾人可陳述……

Judging from the above, one may state...

（5）基於上述理由，吾人可

For reasons mentioned above, one may...

（6）最可能的解釋是……

The most likely explanation is that...

（7）這個結果需要更多的說明

This result requires some further explanations.

（8）A給（... B）一個進一步說明

（... A) gives a further account of (... B) .

（9）原因 A 可說明 B 結果

A (His sickness) may account for B (his absence）

3. 本文的適用範圍與限制條件：提醒採用本結果去推廣者，需注意適用

範圍與限制條件。有時刻意隱瞞不足點、適用範圍與限制條件，是相

當不智。但是，隨後仍要再強調本文其他方面的特色。

Notwithstanding its limitation, this study does suggest...

However, these problems could be solved if we consider...

至於時態，使用過去式或現在式動詞時態或助動詞＋V均可。常用參考「套裝句型」：

（1）本文的一些限制爲……

Some limitations of this study are...

（2）注意本文僅探討（著重於）……

Note that this study has examined (or concentrated on) only...

（3）注意在……我們的資料是有限的

Note that this paper has only limited information on...

=Note that the information on... is limited.

（4）因此，我們無法肯定說……

Therefore, one cannot say for certain whether...

（5）本研究設計並不允許我們去評估……，不過，截至目前卻可計算……

This study design did not allow anyone to evaluate... , but, so far one could determine...

（6）本研究所獲得結果，可適用到……情況：

The result obtained may apply to the case of...

（7）我們必須指出我們無法……

We have to point out that we cannot... （儘量避免使用第一人稱）

= Notably, this article cannot... （較含蓄的第三人稱）

（8）B情況亦同樣適用

The same is true of the case (B)

（9）有一重要點要注意，就是……將不一定提供最佳……，但是……

It is important to note that... will not necessarily provide the best... , but...

（10）相反情形適用於……

The converse holds for...

（11）尚有許多事留待進行

Much still remains to be done.

4. 未來可行的研究與建議：提供讀者進一步研究的方向與可行的主題，使用未來式動詞時態或助動詞＋V均可。常用參考「套裝句型」：

（1）未來進一步研究在……

A further study will be done on...

（2）有進一步研究空間

There is room for further investigation.

（3）關於未來進一步研究……可作如下建議

The following recommendations may be made for the future further study on...

（4）下列各建議將作為未來進一步研究

The following suggestions will be left as future researches.

（5）為證實本分析模式，將來進一步實驗是必需的

To confirm the analytical model, one may conduct (= carry out) further experiments in the future.

（6）本研究在未來飛機而言相當重要；下一代 TC 系統或許因而不同於今日

This may be particularly important as future aircraft and the next-generation TC system are likely to be very different from Today's.

七、承認與感謝辭（Acknowledgements）

由機關或計畫財力支持的研究通常要作承認性聲明與感謝辭，有時在文章送審時，有些評審者（Reviewer）會提供一些建議或討論，也可表示謝意。其表現範例如下：

1. 以上研究係由……資助。

The above research was funded by...

2. 本文係部分由……資助（計畫編號……）。

The work was partially supported by... (Grant No... .)

3. 本文由ＮＳＣ計畫編號……資助。

This work was supported by grant No... . from NSC.

4. 本研究財力係由中華民國國科會計畫（編號……）資助。

This study was financially supported by NSC of R.O.C (grant No... .)

5. 作者感謝地承受來自國科會，計畫編號……的資助本研究。

The authors gratefully acknowledge support for this study from the NSC , project No... .

6. 作者感激地承認……機構支持本研究進行。

The authors acknowledge gratefully the support given by... Institute, for this ongoing research.

7. 作者要感謝楊教授在本研究期間提出許多有益建議。

The authors wish to thank Professor Young for many helpful suggestions during the course of this work.

8. 作者感激地承認與王博士數次有益的討論。

Several helpful discussions with Dr. Wang are gratefully acknowledged.

9. 如下表示 「我要感謝（某人）……」常用參考「套裝句型」：……代表（什麼事）：

（1）寶貴的建議：for valuable advicefor

（2）有幫助的提議：helpful suggestions

（3）寶貴的意見與評論：for valuable comments and criticisms

（4）提供我資料：for providing me with the materials

（5）他協助搜集資料：for his assistance in collecting the information

（6）慷慨財力支援：for generous financial assistance

例如：I wish (=would like to) thank (somebody) for... (something）.

例如：I wish to express my gratitude to (somebody）for... (something）.

例如：My (special) thanks are due to (somebody) for... (something）.

例如：I am indebted to (somebody) for... (something）.

例如：I gratefully acknowledge support for this study from some institute.

☆ 讀者心得增補筆記欄 ☆

參

口頭發表篇

How to Make an Effective Oral Presentation

今年（94年）6月底參加在歐洲波蘭舉行第四屆國際熱學研討會，榮幸被指定為分組主持人，筆者 在國內也主持過數場經驗，但仍發現有不少點差異，值得我們注意與學習。茲分享如下：

一、準備Power Point 講稿的基本原則：簡潔、有效與清晰

1. 暗色藍底背景下，使用白色或黃色文字；或者反過來亮色（淡黃色系）底背景下，使用黑色或深藍色文字。根據專家經驗為較舒適的文字稿。避免紅綠配在一張，因此為常見色盲的盲點。

2. 記得務必把重點用不同亮色或粗黑體字強調出來，不宜超過三色，亦不宜採畫底線方式。但是超連接，常使用畫底線方式進入。

3. 字體大小為24點左右，不宜小於18點單位。中文大標題可使用30點。英文大標題用36點。

4. 儘量使用流程方塊圖呈現，配合箭頭，少用全文字稿。

5. 每張文字稿最好不超過 7 行，每行英文字大約不超過 6 字，避免太擠。

6. 第一張爲演講主題與服務的大學與職稱；第二張爲演講大綱
   （Outline）；第三張爲背景或引言（Introduction），包 括最重要文獻
   回顧，不宜太多，……；最後一張爲謝謝觀眾的耐心聽講。（Thank
   you for your patience （ or attention）!）

7. 注意口頭報告並不等於書面報告而是精選，因此不是全部論文均要顯
   現出來，例如：參考文獻或符號說明均不用。又如可在引言中，放置
   較引人興趣的背景、相片圖或簡短電影。文獻回顧，只提重要作者、
   年代與發現點，不必完整句子。若引用別人圖、相片時，切記在右下
   角著明參考出處。

8. 歡迎參考使用本書背後附加光碟，換成爲你的資料即可。

二、演講時基本原則與技巧

1. 以清晰、中等速度演講，因爲我們的英文並不道地，寧可講慢一點，
   讓人聽得懂最要緊；並配合雷射筆或加上手勢爲宜。（請自備搖控換
   頁與雷射筆，尤其在東歐）

2. 避免單一聲調，每遇到新的階段或論點，可提高聲調大聲一點。

3. 應站直，避免頻頻走動，儘量使用遙控雷射筆（可自備）換頁。

4. 應站在螢光幕的一側邊，儘量靠近觀眾。

5. 不要因讀螢幕訊息文字而背對觀眾太久，可藉轉頭配合雷射筆導引
   後，及時再面向觀眾繼續演講。

6. 保持眼光自然地投射到大部分會眾，且儘量讓眼光往最後一排投射。大約每位停留數秒即可，避免注視同一位太久。較害羞內向的人，可技巧地把眼光稍微調在大部分會眾上面一點點，應可感覺自然一點。

7. 最重要一點欲達到享受不同場合演講，就是放清鬆自己避免緊張，同時你表現愈肯定自信，愈能說服觀眾其實觀眾是站在你這一邊，想要了解並且從事相關研究。

三、演講遭遇問題時的處置技巧

1. 若一開始出現緊張，可先深呼吸或喝口水，然後微笑面向觀眾，即可察覺觀眾和善的眼神且微笑回報，如此開始講演應可改善緊張情緒。記得不必為緊張而道歉，反而更加讓人注意到。把焦點調向觀眾與你的訊息；而非你本身即可減少緊張。

2. 若欲確定觀眾有否跟上，可問會眾。

「Is that clear?」或「Does that make sense?」

應避免使用 「You know?」或「You see?」的口頭禪。

3. 面對觀眾提出問題時，可先思索一下後才回答；若聽不清楚可禮貌要求對方再陳述其問題。

「Pardon me!」或「I beg your pardon」

I just missed that. Could you say it again, please？

I didn't catch that. Could you repeat it slowly, please?

確定其所提的真正問題後才回答。

或者，往發問者走近點，然後提出你聽到的部分並說：Do you mean "…"？

4. 若無法回答觀眾所提出問題，千萬不要不反應站著發呆可答說:我目前沒有此方面資料，我回去研究看，再答覆你。或者，直接表明你無法回答或會後再討論。

"May we discuss your question after this session?"

不用道歉。此時，亦可徵詢會眾對此問題看法與意見。

"May I invite any suggestion for this question?"

5. 問題討論時，要記得時間快到時提醒觀眾。

"We're almost out-of-time. I can take one more quick question."

四、國際研討會時，英文表達的實際應用範例

1. 當小組主持人介紹你演講者與題目後，上台第一句話時，記得面帶微笑且點頭地說出：「Thank you, Mr. Chairman」

2. 然後等字幕顯示出你的演講題目與服務單位職稱後，開始演講，首先仍再度陳述演講題目（……）：

Good Morning, Ladies and Gentlemen, I am gonna talk about (...)

Well, I'd like to present my topic on (...)

3. 介紹完演講主題，第二張通常為預告（Preview）演講大綱（Outline），例如：如下的 Power point：

Outline:

• Introduction

• Modeling

• Results and Dissassion

• Conclusion

口頭可大致如下帶過來：

I will give this presentation in (four) parts (Let's take a quick look at the outline of my presentation here). First, Introduction, Second, Modeling, Third, Results; Finally, Conclusion.

4. 進入另一階段之承接用語：

Now, let's move on (or, shift; look at) to the (introduction, result, conclusion,...) , now, we come to next item.

Next, I am gonna present the （modeling, result, conclusion,..).

5. 進行結果圖表時，記得要說出橫座標與縱座標變數。

（1）What I am showing here is the result or figure of (...), its Y-coordinate denotes... and X-coordinate is...

（2） Here is the result of...

（3） What you see here is...

（4） The interesting or important result here is...

等四種說明結果圖；時間許可的話，應說明其變化趨勢與原因。

6. 演講最後一部分，是歸納你今天所講的重點，即進入結論，表現用

語如下：

（1） Finally, in conclusion, I have (or I'd like to point out the following.

（2） To sum up, we have the following points.

（3） Finally, I'd like to make some concluding remarks for my presentation.

（4） In concluding my presentation here, I'd like to emphasize the

following.

（5） OK, to highlight (recap) the main points (of my talk), I make the

following conclusions.

7. 當演講末了，放出最後一張「Thank you for your kind patience (or

attention) .」順便說出：「Thank you.」。

8. 緊接著主持人會邀請與會者提問題討論：「Thank you (speaker, Prof.

Young). Now, this paper is open for discussion.」或「Now, I'd like to

invite questions (for this paper)」，簡單說出「Any comment (for this

paper) ?」

9. 面對與會者所提問題，可藉你的先前結果圖來回答，同時說：

Well, let's go back to the Fig.（...）

答覆完，亦可確定對方是否明白了而說：

Is that clear (for you)?

10. 若聽不清楚與會者所提問題，欲其重述問題時，應禮貌性說：

Pardon?

Would you please repeat your question again?

11. 若無法回答觀眾所提出問題，可如下回答：

I don't have that information now, but I'll look into it and get back to you.

或者，直接表明你無法回答：

I can't answer your question at this moment, but I'll look into it later on.

不用道歉。此時主持人通常會幫你徵詢其他與會者看法。

May I invite any suggestion for this question?

五、國際研討會若有幸被指定為分組主持人 (Session Chairman)

　　是一種榮譽；然而，必須於會前先閱讀，在這小組所有將發表者的背景資料，方便研討會時作介紹。當然，更要注意講出合適的英文，大致過程如下：

1. 會議開始時首先自我介紹 （Opening and Welcome） 如下：各位先生、女士：歡迎參與本（小組）研討，我是（某某人），來自於（臺灣），很榮幸主持這一節研討會。

Ladies and Gentlemen: Welcome to this session, I am (Sam Yang), from (Taiwan). First, I would like to thank the committee for giving me this opportunity to be with you. It's my honor (or It's a great pleasure) to chair this session. (or simply say "I will chair this session.")

2. 接著，大致說明每位演講者演講時間與討論時間如下：首先，容許我簡單說明一下，本分組研討進行的過程：每位演講者都有20分鐘發表；包括3到5分鐘進行討論。

First of all, let me briefly explain the conference a little, that is, each speaker has twenty minutes to present, including five minutes around to discuss.

3. 事前準備（閱讀）即將發表者的資料後，開始介紹第一位論文發表者的資料，包括姓名、職分 （Prof...、Dr... . ）與來自那裡、甚至研究興趣領域以及講題如下，然後請觀眾一起鼓掌歡迎：

The first speaker is Prof. Kern, from Germany. He earned his Ph. D from Berlin University in 1980. Currently, he is Head of Mechanical engineering. Today, his topic is (...). Now, Ladies and Gentlemen, please join me to welcome Professor Ken and clap big hands.

4. 等第一位演講完畢後，主持人表示謝謝後，開放給予會者提問題如下：

Thank you. Now, this paper is open for discussion.

5. 若剛開始提問題較冷清，主持人須破冰先向演講者提出問題如下：

Well, let me break the ice and ask the speaker a question.

或說也許大家仍有點緊張，容許我先提個問題：

I guess everyone's still kind of uptight. Allow me ask the speaker a question.

6. 接著仍應徵尋是否有其他問題？

Any other question?

7. 主持人必須嚴格控制每位的時間，若每一位演講後，仍遇到許多問題時，主持人必須提醒會眾「因時間快到，只限再提一問題」：

Since we are almost out of time, we can only open one more question.

8. 結束研討會時，主持人仍須謝謝演講者，並宣布結束研討會如下：

I would like to thank our speakers again and close this session here.

Thank you everybody!

六、 個人參加國際研討會的心得摘錄

1. 務必參加歡迎招待晚宴（Welcome Reception），儘量多去認識與會者並交換名片，尤其大會組織幹部包括主席、秘書、與其他分組主持人，通常你可預備一些簡單小抄，介紹你自己資料（或把小抄）給所屬分組主持人；若被選為分組主持人，更需要去搜集，帶便條與筆，請所屬講員親自寫下簡短自我資料，包括來歷、研究專長及榮譽事蹟。若想知道演講者到底是哪一位，可央求大會秘書幫你介紹。讓更多國際學者認識你，無形中提高自己的國際知名度，以後投稿國際期刊具有正面加分效果。千萬不要不好意思，覺得自己英語不如歐美人士，就只顧吃東西後趕快回到旅館房間去看電視。其實，我們臺灣學者英語發音在亞洲內除新加坡、香港外算比較好。記得講慢一點，把重點字清楚的講出來，大部分與會歐美人士都聽得懂，不必擔心，大不了把關鍵字再唸一遍罷了。下列摘錄一些常用慣用語與口語化英語

（1） 高興遇見你！

Nice（=Great） to meet you！

（2） 我必須離開或走了。

I gotta (= have to) leave now.

I'm outta here=I am out of here.

（3） 我將發表下列主題。

I'm gonna present the following topic

（4） 抱歉！我沒有跟上（聽到）你方才所說！

Sorry! I can't catch you. (= Pardon me!)

（5） 你的發表對我很有用。

Your presentation is very handy (= useful) for me.

（6） 之後，我將再次檢查我的數據。

I'll double-check (= re-check or verify) my data later on.

2. 參加別人發表論文時，若對其研究有興趣時，除了可以自備錄音筆錄音外，會後也可禮貌性地請問演講者，是否可把Power point講稿複製給你？因其中含有影片檔是大會論文集所沒有。通常Keynote lecture比較精彩，比較值得錄製。

3. 輪到自己上台發表論文時，等分組主持人介紹你完畢，記得面帶微笑的說出 「Thank you, Mr. Chairman!」 ，然後有信心地唸出你演講主題。接著，務必把你演講大綱（Outline）陳述出來。讓與會者事先了解你講題大概內容，有助於他們抓得到你想要發表的論文。如此分組主席人也便於幫你掌控時間，或提醒你時間到了沒？記得請務必在分配時間內完成論文發表，千萬不要越時。影響其他的之發表，相當不得體。

4. 同樣，若有幸被指定為分組主持人，首要任務也是在時間分配與掌控。可一開始就事先說明清楚，通常大會議程也有分配，只要再強調一次即可。然後於會中，每位演講者時間快到幾分鐘，提醒他說「Excuse me! Two minutes to go! 」或「we are almost out of time」；另外，每次介紹完演講者，記得邀請與會者一起歡迎與帶頭鼓掌。「Please join me to welcome Prof.... and clap.」；當每位演講完畢，務必邀請與會者提出疑問。「Now, this topic is open for discussion」，當第一位提出疑問後，應禮貌地再徵詢其他會眾說「Any other question?」

5. 必參加最後一天總結討論，大會主席會歸納今年在該研討會發表的論文重要發現與成果，並提出未來研究方向與主題，同時與會者亦提出議題討論，相當值得參與。譬如說，此次國際熱學研討會提出的未來研究方向與主題為微尺寸的沸騰與凝結熱傳。（Micro scale in Heat Transfer-Boiling and Condensation）。

6. 這次參加波蘭舉行的第四屆國際熱學研討會為中型規模，限定熱流與相變化熱傳領域主題，參與各國學者連論文壁報張貼者合計大約160人。如同一般國際研討會一樣，需自付了旅館住宿費 （含早餐每天2000元台幣）；至於研討會註冊費為歐員500元，不過它包含五天中、晚餐。由於中、晚餐均在旅館內一起用餐；另外，大會還特別免費招

待安排一天城堡遊覽與半天城市參觀，彼此互動相當好，感覺蠻溫馨，幾乎認識每一位參與者，因此結識不少國際朋友。還被邀請參觀主辦大學研究概況，並進一步談及商雙方日後可能交流。會後還與主辦大學系主任與同事，一起開車至波蘭首都華沙與前首都克拉刻等名勝旅遊四天。當然我也邀請他們至臺灣參加研討會，收穫良多！值得一提的是，有一位即將拿到博士學位的波蘭年青人，問我們國內是否會聘請博士後研究人員？

7. 附錄二為筆者刊登在 2005 年第四屆國際熱學研討會的發表論文至於當時口頭發表之 Power Point 稿與主持會議影片，為供讀者參考，收錄成光碟片置於書背後面，由於複製技術欠佳關係，影音不甚清楚。故詳細有關主持演講技巧，仍請參閱前面「五、」部分的文字說明。

8. 由於複製技術欠佳關係，影音不甚清楚，大致摘錄當時重要講詞如下：

Good morning, Ladies and Gentlemen! Welcome to the final session of Heat 2005 Conference. I'm Sam Yang, from Taiwan. I am very happy to have this opportunity to chair this session. I really enjoy attending this international conference. There is a famous slang saying "Good wine always reserves in the bottom." So, you may expect to have a great lecture at this final session.

Now, the first Keynote speaker is Prof. Vasilieve, from Belarus. He is head of porous media Lab, Luikov Heat and Mass Transfer Institute. Prof. Vasilieve earned his Ph. D degree from Minsk Polytechnic Institute. So far, he published 11 books and near 390 journal and conference papers. He is a member of the Editorial board of the Journal of Applied Thermal Engineering and also the invited Editor of J. of Thermal Science. He received the Soviet Union State award and award of the Council of Ministers, one gold and two silver medals... and so on.

Today, the topic of his keynote lecture is "Micro and miniature heat pipes for electronic components cooling". Now, Ladies and Gentlemen, please join me to welcome Prof. Vasilieve.

(After Prof. Vasilieve's presentation) For the moment, this paper is open for question. (When any attendant raised his hand, I passed my microphone to him and say) "Please!" (Later on) "Any other question?" ; "Since we're almost out of time, we can take one more question." (At the end) "Thank Prof. Vasilieve!"

Next, let's move on to the second lecture presented by Dr. Kern, from Germany. Dr. Kern earned his Ph. D degree from Darmstadt University of Technology, Germany, 2001. His current research of interest is heat and mass transfer in nucleate boiling of pure substance and binary mixtures. Since 2005, he joined Bayer as R & D engineer. Today, his lecture's topic is "A numerical model for vapor bubble nucleation" Now, Ladies and Gentlemen, please join me to welcome Dr. Kern.

(Since the presentation time for Dr. Kern is almost over, I give him a hint)

"Excuse me! Two minutes to go!" (Later on) Thank Dr. Kern! Now, we are open for discussion. Any question. "Please" . Any other question. "Please."

Ok, the third lecture is presented by Prof. Broniarz-Press, from Poland. She is Head of Division of Chemical Engineering and Equipment, Poznan University of Technology. She earned her Ph. D. degree from Poznan University of Technology in 1977 and also Dr. degree in Science, from Warsaw University of Technology in 1993. Her scientific areas of interest are （1） Falling liquid film phenomena （2） Enhancement of heat and mass transfer in film and spray columns （3） Multiphase flows.

Her lecture's topic today is "Local value of heat transfer coefficient for shear-thinning fluids in agitated vessels" . Now, Ladies and Gentlemen, please join me to welcome Prof. Broniarz-Press.

(Give her time up hint) "Excuse me! One minute to go!" (After

her presentation) Thank Prof. Broniarz-Press! Now, we are open for discussion. Since we are almost out of time, we just take one question here. "Please." ...

Finally, I would like to thank our speakers again and close this session here. Thank you everybody!

☆ 讀者心得增補筆記欄 ☆

七、中國學生口語上常見不當字或表錯意思的句子

1. Is this seat empty?（中式）

   Is this seat taken?

2. Your overcoat is broken.（中式）

   Your overcoat is torn.（美式）

3. Esther didn't make a fault anyway.（中式用字不當）

   Esther didn't make a mistake anyway.

4. The kid is very dangerous while playing in the street.（中式誤寫成危險人物，而非處在危險中）

   The kid is in great danger while playing in the street.

   It is very dangerous for that kid to play in the street.

5. Jason was painful when his girlfriend left him.（中式）

   Jason was in pain when his girlfriend left him.

   Jason felt pained when his girlfriend left him.

6. I recommend you to take a long vacation.（中式）

   I recommend that you take a long vacation.

7. It is still bright outside.（中式）

It is still light outside.

8. Different from you, she is proficient in English.（中式）

Unlike you, she is proficient in English.

9. Little children are difficult to understand your words.（中式錯）

It is difficult for children to understand your words.

10. Don't expect him too much.（中式）

Don't expect too much from (of) him.

11. I know her face.（中式）

I know her by sight.

12. I forget my book in the house.（中式表錯意思）

I left my book in the house.

13. Do you have free time?（中式）

Are you free?

14. The sun rises from the East.（中式）

The sun rises in the East.

15. Let's read from page 5.（中式表錯意思）

Let's read at (on) page 5.

16. The boy's temperature went down.（中式用字不當）

   The boy's temperature came down.

17. Today's newspaper has my son's articles on Taiwan.（中式用字不當）

   Today's newspaper carries my son's articles on Taiwan.

18. Give him money, if you have.（中式用字不當）

   Give him money, if you have any.

19. How heavy are you?（中式用字不當）

   How much do you weigh?

20. This is the way how I did it.（中式用字不當）

   This is how I did it. or This is the way I did it.

21. How do you think about (=of) Chinese culture?（中式）

   What do you think about (=of) Chinese culture?

22. This thing reaches a limit in my patience.（中式用字不當）

   This thing reaches a limit to my patience.

23. Is this house insured for fire?（中式用字不當）

   Is this house insured against fire?

24. He was first prize.（中式用字不當）

   He took first prize.

25. Please keep the right.（中式用字不當）

    Please keep to the right.

26. The train was late about an hour.（中式）

    The train was about an hour late.

27. It is my first time to go abroad.（中式）

    It is the first time I go abroad.

28. This room is narrow.（中式）

    This room is small.

29. While walking along the beach, I met my friend.（中式）

    While walking along the beach, I met a friend of mine.

30. This is the key of your room.（中式）

    This is the key to your room.

31. I am going to take a two-year course of Mathematics.（中式）

    I am going to take a two-year course in Mathematics.

32. I am a student of UCLA.（中式）

    I am a student at UCLA.

33. I saw it on the yesterday's newspapers.（中式）

    I read it in the yesterday's newspapers.

34. What is the total sum?（中式）總共多少錢？

How much does it come to?

35. You have wide shoulders.（中式）你可承擔重任。

You have broad shoulders.

36. I bought this book with 220 dollars.（中式）

I bought this book for 220 dollars.

37. He played all this Sunday without working.（中式）

He played all this Sunday instead of working.

38. I felt very difficult to deal with this mathematical problem.（中式）

I found it very difficult to deal with this mathematical problem.

It was very difficult for me to deal with this mathematical problem.

39. Thanks to see me.（中式）

Thanks for dropping by.

40. We had a lot of difficulty to find the parking place.（中式）

We had a lot of difficulty (in) finding the parking place.

41. Please give me a detail description of the accident.（中式）

Please give me a detailed description of the accident.

Please give me (all) the details of the accident.

Please describe the accident in detail.

附錄一
投稿書信篇

一、電子上傳投稿的封面書信 (Covering letter) 參考範例

Date on June 8th, 05

Professor First Last

Editor-in-Chief

Mailing Address

Dear Professor Last,

Attached please find my manuscript entitled,"... " submitted for possible publication in Journal of... (or, to International Conference of... for possible presentation).

"Attached please find my manuscript entitled, "... " to be published in Journal of... if possible."

This manuscript is entirely original, and has not been considered or published in any other organizations or elsewhere. Your acknowledgement will be highly appreciated. Thank you.

Sincerely yours,

Samuel Yang, Ph.D

Professor

Department of Mold and Die Engineering

National Kaohsiung University of Applied Sciences

Kaohsiung, 807

TAIWAN (R. O. C.)

二、主編確認收到回函

Re T123 "..."

Dear Prof. Samuel Yang,

This is to acknowledge receipt of the following manuscript :

Paper reference no. T123 "..."

You will be notified via email when the review of this manuscript is completed or available. Please refer to the paper number in any communications regarding your manuscript.

Sincerely,

Editor-in-Chief

三、查詢審稿進度

Date on Nov. 1st, 05

Paper reference no. ： T123

Dear Pro. AAA, Editor,

I am writing you concerning the status of my paper referenced above.

Recently, I checked the status of my manuscript entitled, "... ", T123, submitted for possible publication in Journal of... and found the review record remained "Awaiting Reviewer Assignment".

Your acknowledgement will be highly appreciated.

Best wishes,

Samuel Yang, Ph. D

Professor

Department of Mold and Die Engineering

National Kaohsiung University of Applied Sciences

Kaohsiung, 807

TAIWAN (R. O. C.)

四、要求修改並回覆函

Re : T123 "... "

Dear Editor or Prof. AAA,

Attached please find the revised manuscript referenced above, together with "Response to Reviewers Comments".

(Attached please find our response to Reviewers comments and the revised text to accommodate Reviewers comments.)

Your acknowledgement will be highly appreciated. Thank you.

Sincerely yours,

Samuel Yang, Ph. D

Professor

Department of Mold and Die Engineering

National Kaohsiung University of Applied Sciences

Kaohsiuing, 807

TAIWAN (R. O. C.)

Response to Reviewers and Editor

Paper reference no. : T123

Title : "... "

[Reviewer #1 Comments]

1...

2...

3...

[Response to Reviewer #1]

1...

2...

3...

[Reviewer #2 Comments]

1...

2...

[Response to Reviewer #2]

1...

2...

五、小幅度修改論文之接受函

Dear Prof. Samuel Yang,

The review of your manuscript entitled, "... ", T123, has been completed. The reviewers were positive and recommended publishing with minor revisions. (or, The editorial review board feels that the manuscript requires a few minor revisions before it can be published in the Journal of... .) Once sending back the next revision, your manuscript will be ready for publication.

Thank you for your interest in publishing in the Journal of...

Sincerely yours,

Prof. AAA, BBB

Editor

Journal of...

☆ 讀者心得增補筆記欄 ☆

附錄二
HEAT 2005 國際研討會－實例

HEAT2005

Gdansk, Poland
June 26-30, 2005

4th INTERNATIONAL CONFERENCE ON TRANSPORT PHENOMENA IN MULTIPHASE SYSTEMS

EFFECT OF EDDY DIFFUSIVITY ON TURBULENT FILM CONDENSATION OUTSIDE A HORIZONTAL TUBE

Sheng-An YANG1, Yan-Ting LIN2

1Professor, Department of Mold and Die Engineering, National Kaohsiung
University of Applied Sciences, Kaohsiung 807, TAIWAN, E-mail : samyang@cc.kuas.edu.tw
2Graduate student, Department of Mold and Die Engineering, National Kaohsiung
University of Applied Sciences, Kaohsiung 807, TAIWAN, E-mail : a091316102@cc.kuas.edu.tw

ABSTRACT

The effect of eddy diffusivity upon the turbulent film condensation of saturated vapor flowing downward onto a horizontal isothermal circular tube is performed theoretically by employing the Hilpert semi-empirical model. The interfacial shear of the vapor from laminar flow to turbulent flow is evaluated with help of potential flow theory. The transition region or the separation point of condensate film is also studied for the following different dominant parameters, including Prandtl number, Reynolds number, sub-cooling parameters and system pressure parameter. The condensate film flow and the heat transfer characteristics under the effects of eddy diffusivity and the above mentioned parameters are investigated. The present result shows in better agreement with the experimental data than the previous theoretical modes do.

Keywords: Turbulent, Film Condensation, Eddy Diffusivity Effect, Horizontal Tube
NOMENCLATURE

F   dimensionless inverse vapor velpcity parameter, $2/(\text{Fr S})$

Fr   Froude number, u_∞^2 / gR

Gr   Grashof number, $\left(\dfrac{gR^3}{v_l^2}\right)\left(\dfrac{\rho_l - \rho_v}{\rho_l}\right)$

h_{fg} latent heat of condensate

Pr   Prandtl number, v / α

R   radius of horizontal tube

$\overline{St}$ Stanton number $\dfrac{\overline{Nu}}{\text{Re}_v \, \text{Pr}}$

T^+ dimensionless temperature, $(\overline{T_{sat}} - \overline{T_w})/(\overline{T_{sat}} - \overline{T_w})$

u_e the tangential vapor velocity at the edge of the boundary layer,

u^* shear velocity, $(\tau_w / \rho_l)^{1/2}$

y^+ dimensionless distance normal to

Re_l, Re_v Reynolds number,
$u_\infty D/v_l$, $u_\infty D/v_v$

Re^* shear Reynolds, $\text{Re}^+/Gr^{1/3}$

Re^+ shear Reynolds, parameter,
Ru^*/v_l

S sub-cooling parameter,
$C_P(\overline{T_{sat}}-\overline{T_w})/(h_{fg}\,\text{Pr})$

ε_M momentum eddy diffusivity

ε_H thermal eddy diffusivity

v kinematic viscosity

ρ density

the circular tube wall, yu^*/v_l

δ^+ dimensionless film thickness, $\delta u^*/v_l$

φ interfacial shear parameter,

$$2^n\pi C\left(\frac{\rho_v}{\rho_l}\right)\left(\frac{v_l}{v_v}\right)^{n-1}Gr^{(3n-1)/6}$$

c critical condition

l condensate film

m mean valus

Subscripts

1. INTRODUCTION

Film condensation heat transfer on a horizontal tube has been extensively investigated because of its applications in air conditioning system, condenser, electronic system cooling, etc. For laminar film condensation with constant properties and ignoring the vapor velocity, the assumption of the simple Nusselt theory [1] have been provided in later and more complete studies to be basically accurate. In 1966, Shekriladze and Gomelauri [2] first considered forced convection film condensation from a vapor flowing downward to a horizontal circular tube, and obtained numerical solutions by utilizing the asymptotic shear stress at the interface. Later, Rose[3] and Hsu and Yang [4] took further account of the pressure gradient upon the condensation heat transfer on a horizontal circular tube using the Shekriladze and Gomelauri method. All the above-mentioned analyses are in fairly good agreement with experimental data for low vapor velocities (F>1) . However, they did not give satisfactory results for condensate film in wave/turbulent situation or under high vapor velocity.

Generally speaking, the difference between the theoretical and experimental results for high-vapor velocities has often been attributed to turbulence in the liquid film and formation of ripples at the surface of liquid film due to vapor shear. To modify this difference, Sarma et al. [5] first used Kato's model [6] of eddy diffusivity and Hilpert's semi-empirical model in the condensate film and assumed that the friction coefficient at liquid vapor interface is identical to that in vapor flow. They found that the results were in good agreement with experimental data relating to the condensation of steam flowing under a wave regime. Nevertheless, the Nusselt number of Sarma's work is still larger than experimental data under turbulent saturated vapor (F =0.001... 0.1) . More recently, Homescu and Panday[7] used an implicit scheme to solve the film condensation on an isothermal horizontal tube under pure vapors flowing vertically and obtained the numerical solution of coupled liquid-vapor interface for Kato's model[6] in liquid phase and Pletcher's model[8] in vapor phase. They also compared their results with Michael et al.[9] and Honda et al.[10] experimental results

133

and found in better agreement than Sarma et al[5] prediction did, when the vapor velocity is not too high, i.e. the dimensionless inverse vapor velocity, F, is not too small. However, the two–phase coupled boundary layer equations seem tedious in numerical calculation. Meanwhile, the mean heat transfer coefficients in both Sarma et al. [5] and Homescu and Panday [7] tend to go up sharply as F is decreasing to 0.001. However, the mean heat transfer coefficients in the previous experimental work show down-trend as F is decreasing to 0.001. This significant difference may be attributed to the separation of condensate film missed in the both analyses.

For simplicity and efficient evaluation, we direct our attention toward a single-phase model and first introduce an eddy diffusivity effect into the interface energy balance relation. Owing to the eddy diffusivity effect included, the separation of the condensate film does happen in the present analysis. The analysis may be regarded as an extended version of the analysis proposed by Sarma et al.[5] for turbulent film condensation. Basically, it is also designed to improve the difference in very high vapor flow velocities between the previous theoretical result and experiment data.

2. ANALYSIS

Figure 1 illustrates schematically a physical model and coordinate system of condensate film along an isothermal tube. The curvilinear coordinate (x, y) is aligned along the circular tube wall surface and its normal. Outside the condensate layer, a pure saturated vapor flows at temperature and at uniform velocity . The tube wall surface temperature is below the saturation temperature. A thin condensate film is formed and flows under the influence of gravity, interfacial shear and physical properties.

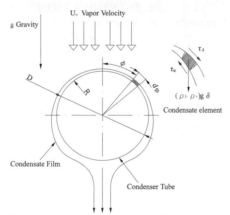

Fig.1. Physical model and coordinate system

English
Technical
Articles

The conservation equations governing condensate flow are

$$\bar{u}\frac{\partial \bar{T}}{\partial x}+\bar{v}\frac{\partial \bar{T}}{\partial y}=\frac{d}{dy}\left[(\alpha+\varepsilon_{11})\frac{d\bar{T}}{dy}\right] \tag{1}$$

$$\tau_w = g\delta(\rho_l - \rho_v)\sin\phi+\tau_\delta \tag{2}$$

$$\frac{d}{Rd\phi}\int_0^\delta \rho_l\bar{u}dy=\frac{k_l}{h_{fg}}\frac{d\bar{T}}{dy}\bigg|_{y=0} \tag{3}$$

The boundary conditions are

$$x = 0 \ ; \ \bar{u} = 0; \tag{4}$$

$$y = 0 \ ; \ \bar{u}=\bar{v}=0, \ T=T_w \tag{5}$$

$$y = \delta \ ; \ \frac{\partial \bar{u}}{\partial y}=0, \ T=T_{sat} \tag{6}$$

Note that Eq. (2), reflects a force balance of gravity, wall shear and interfacial vapor shear effects. Eq. (3) is an energy balance between the latent heat released at the interface from condensate film to the horizontal tube wall surface.

For a horizontal tube in external flow, the mean Nusselt number can be stated in terms of Prandtl and Reynolds number by using a Hilpert semi-empirical model, as seen in Incropera and DeWitt [11].

$$\overline{Nu}=C\,\mathrm{Re}_v^{\,n}\,\mathrm{Pr}^{1/3} \tag{7}$$

where the constants C and
n are listed in [11]. Further, using Colburn's analogy [11], one has

$$\frac{\bar{f}}{2}=\overline{St}\,\mathrm{Pr}^{2/3} \tag{8}$$

From Eq. (7) and Eq. (8), we have the mean friction coefficient as

$$\bar{f}=2C\,\mathrm{Re}_v^{\,n-1} \tag{9}$$

As mentioned in Homescu and Panday's [7], we may define local friction coefficient in terms of a Sin function for a circular tube.

$$f_\phi = C\pi(\text{Re}_v^{n-1})\sin\phi \tag{10}$$

The local skin shear stress is defined as

$$\tau_\delta = \frac{1}{2}(\rho_v)(u_e^2)f_\phi \tag{11}$$

By potential flow theory for a uniform flow with velocity past a horizontal tube, one may derive the vapor velocity at the edge of boundary layer as

$$u_e = 2u_\infty \sin\phi \tag{12}$$

From Eqs. (10-12), the vapor-liquid interfacial shear stress can be obtained

$$\tau_\delta = 2(C)(\pi)(\rho_v)(u_\infty^2)(\text{Re}_v^{n-1})\sin^3\phi \tag{13}$$

Finally, Eq. (2) is rewritten as follows

$$\tau_w = g\delta(\rho_l - \rho_v)\sin\phi + 2(C)(\pi)(\rho_v)(u_\infty^2)(\text{Re}_v^{n-1})\sin^3\phi \tag{14}$$

Since the condensate film sufficiently closes to the solid wall, the turbulent conduction across the condensate film is more significant than the convective component. As mentioned in Bejan [12], the energy equation (Eq. (1)) with assuming = 1 reduces to

$$\frac{d}{dy}\left[\left(1 + \frac{\varepsilon_M}{v_l}\text{Pr}\right)\frac{d\overline{T}}{dy}\right] = 0 \tag{15}$$

By introducing the dimensionless groupings, Eqs. (3), (14) and (15) can be restated as follows

$$\frac{\partial}{\partial \phi} \int_0^{\delta^+} (u^+)dy^+ = (S)(Re^*)\left(1+\frac{\varepsilon_M}{v_l}\Pr\right)(Gr^{1/3})\frac{\partial T^+}{\partial y^+}\bigg|_{y^+=0} \qquad (16)$$

$$(Re^*)^3 = \delta^+ \sin\phi + (Re^*)(\varphi)(Fr)^{(n+1)/2}\sin^3\phi \qquad (17)$$

$$\frac{d}{dy^+}\left[\left(1+\frac{\varepsilon_M}{v_l}\Pr\right)\frac{d\bar{T}^+}{dy^+}\right]=0, \qquad (18)$$

with the following dimensionless boundary conditions :

$$x^+ = 0 ; \quad u^+ = 0 \qquad (19)$$
$$y^+ = 0 ; u^+ = v^+ = 0, \ T^+ = 0 \qquad (20)$$
$$y^+ = \delta^+; \ \frac{\partial u^+}{\partial y} = 0, \ T^+ = 1 \qquad (21)$$

Before proceeding to obtain
the solution of Eq. (16) and thence to calculate the velocity profile in condensate film, based on the assumption, the universal velocity distribution is being used in the estimation of discharge rate of the condensate at any angular location, we may assume that   is of the same order as   and be considered as a valid approximation. As seen in Bejan [12], the velocity profile of condensate film can be obtained from

$$\frac{\partial u^+}{\partial y^+} = \left(1+\frac{\varepsilon_M}{v_l}\right)^{-1} \qquad (22)$$

It is necessary to assume the eddy diffusivity of turbulence to solve the governing equations (18) and (22). Kato proposed the following equation to predict the eddy diffusivity expression

$$\frac{\varepsilon_M}{v_l} = 0.4y^+[1-\exp(-0.0017y^{+2})] \qquad (23)$$

Then, combining Eqs. (19), (22)

and (23) for temperature gradient in the close vicinity of the tube, yields

$$\left.\frac{\partial T^+}{\partial y^+}\right)_{y^+=0} = \left\{1+\Pr\left[0.4y^+\left(1-e^{\left(-0.0017y^{+2}\right)}\right)\right]\left[\int_0^{\delta^+}\frac{dy^+}{1+\Pr\left[0.4y^+\left(1-e^{\left(-0.0017y^{+2}\right)}\right)\right]}\right]\right\}^{-1} \quad (24)$$

The
dimensionless local heat transfer coefficient may be expressed as

$$Nu = \mathrm{Re}^+\left.\frac{dT^+}{dy^+}\right|_{y^+=0} \quad (25)$$

$$\frac{Nu}{\mathrm{Re}_l^{1/2}} = \sqrt{2}\left.\frac{\partial T^+}{\partial y^+}\right)_{y^+=0}\left(\frac{Gr^{\frac{1}{3}}}{Fr}\right)^{\frac{1}{4}}\mathrm{Re}^* \quad (26)$$

The mean heat transfer coefficient is evaluated by integrating Eq. (26)

$$\frac{\overline{Nu}}{\mathrm{Re}_l^{1/2}} = \frac{\sqrt{2}}{\pi}\left(\frac{Gr^{\frac{1}{3}}}{Fr}\right)^{\frac{1}{4}}\int_0^{\pi}\left.\frac{\partial T^+}{\partial y^+}\right)_{y^+=0}\mathrm{Re}^*\,d\phi \quad (27)$$

3. RESULTS AND DISCUSSION

1.1 Flow Hydrodynamics of Condensate Film

Figures 2a and 2b show the dimensionless film thickness profiles around the periphery of circular tube for different parameters including semi-empirical n (power of Reynolds) , system pressure , sub-cooling S, Prandtl number Pr and Froude number Fr. Since the effect of eddy diffusivity is taken into account in the present study, it is obviously seen that the condensate film will separate from the tube wall, which is quite different from the previous work by Sarma et al. [5]. This condensate film separation will occur once sub-cooling effect parameter "S" reaches a certain value, like S=0.05 in Fig.2a.

Meanwhile, the higher Fr and the system pressure parameter   will be advantageous to separation occurring, as seen in Fig.2a and 2b respectively.

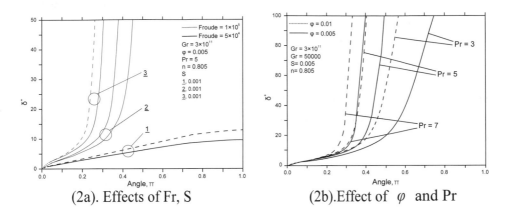

<table>
<tr><td>(2a). Effects of Fr, S</td><td>(2b).Effect of φ and Pr</td></tr>
</table>

Fig.2. Dimensionless local film thickness around periphery of tube

3.2 Characteristics of Heat Transfer

As far as the mean heat transfer characteristics is concerned, it is seen that the mean heat transfer coefficient is increasing linearly with φ, up to φ =0.01,which locates within the laminar flow zone. After φ >0.01, the condensate film flow becomes turbulent and the mean heat transfer coefficient turns out to be a constant value, as shown in Fig.3.

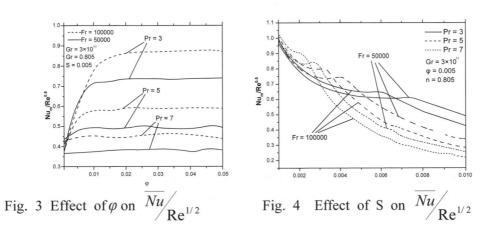

Fig. 3 Effect of φ on $\overline{Nu}/Re^{1/2}$ Fig. 4   Effect of S on $\overline{Nu}/Re^{1/2}$

139

There are two interesting features drawn in Fig.4. Firstly, for the smaller values of S 0.007 (for Pr=3) , the mean heat transfer coefficient is increasing with Fr, which locates in laminar zone. Secondly, for the larger value of S□0.07 for Pr=3, the mean heat transfer coefficient is decreasing with Fr, which locates in turbulent zone.

In Fig.5, it can be seen that there is a broad similarity between Michael's [9] data and the present result. In other words, the mean heat transfer coefficient is increasing with F for laminar flow. But for transition zone, the mean heat transfer is increasing as F is decreasing. It reaches a maximum near F=0.01 for =0.01, followed by a rapid decrease because of turbulent flow. Further, it is to be noted that the present result is rather than nearly constant values for laminar model by Hsu and Yang's solution [4] when F is small.

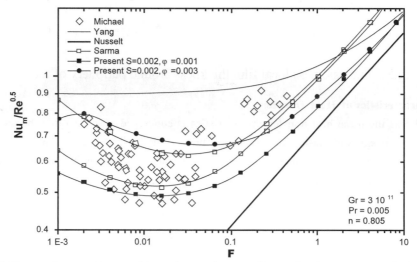

Fig.5. Dependence of mean Nusselt number on dimensionless vapor velocities F

The scatter of the experimental data of Honda et al. [10] for R-113, compared to the present result is seen in Fig. 6. For each case, denoted by 1 and 2 respectively, two lines corresponding to the smallest and largest value of are plotted. The present results for two cases, S=0.025□ and show in better agreement with the experimental data. Above all for the very small values of F, around 0.01, the present trend goes down because of the condensate film separation occurring. However, without taking the eddy diffusivity effect into account in the interface energy equation, like Homescu and Panday [7], and Sarma et al. [5], the mean heat transfer coefficient will go up significantly with decreasing F from 0.01.

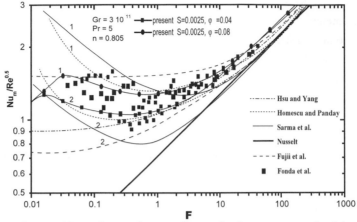

Fig.6. Dependence of mean Nusselt number on dimensionless vapor velocities F

4. CONCLUDING REMARKS

Taking into account the effect of eddy diffusivity in the inter-phase energy equation, the study has confirmed that the condensate film separation does occur. Once the separation occurring, the mean heat transfer coefficient will decrease with an increase in Fr, Pr, and S. Thus, results for the mean Nusselt number were compared satisfactorily well with the existing experimental data obtained by Michael et al.

The mean heat transfer coefficient is increasing with F within laminar zone. However, the lower F or the higher vapor velocity may not make the condensate film flow become turbulent. It must match with the appropriate values of S, and Pr.

5. ACKNOWLEDGMENT

Funding for this investigation was provided by National Science Foundation, ROC. Under grant number NSC 93-2212-E-151-002-.

6. REFERENCES

1. Nusselt, W., Die Oberflachen Kondensation de Wasserdampers, Zeitsehrift desvereines eutsher ingenieure, Vol.60, 1916, pp.541–546.
2. Shekriladze, I. G., and Gomelauri, V. I., Int. J. Heat Mass Transfer, Vol. 9, 1966, pp.581–591.
3. Rose, J. W., Int. J. Heat Mass Transfer, Vol.27, 1984, pp.39-47.
4. Hsu, C. H. and Yang, S. A., Int .J. Heat and Mass Transfer, Vol.42, 1999, pp.2419-2426.
5. Sarma, P. K., Vijayalakshmi, B., Mayinger, F., and Kac, S., Int. J. Heat Mass Transfer, Vol.41, 1998, pp.537-545.

6. Kato, H., Nishiwaki, N. and Hirata, M., Int. J. Heat Mass Transfer, Vol.11, 1967, pp.1117-1125

7. Homescu D. and Panday, P. K., J. Heat Transfer, Vol.121, 1999, pp.874-885.8.Fletcher, R. H., J. of Heat Transfer, 1974, pp.89-94.

9. Michael, A. G., Rose, J. W., and Daniels, L. C., J. of Heat Transfer, Vol.111, 1989, pp.792-797.

10. Honda, H., Nozu, S., Uchima, B. and Fujii, T., Int. J. Heat Mass Transfer, Vol.29, 1986, pp.429-438.

11. Incropera, F. P., and DeWitt, D. P., Introduction to Heat Transfer, 2nd ed., Vol.7, Wiley, New York, 1990, pp. 380-381.

12. Bejan, A., Convection Heat Transfer, 2nd ed., Wiley, Vol.7, New York, 1995, pp.293-324.

☆ 讀者心得增補筆記欄 ☆

附錄三

如何評審科技論文

俗語說：「知己知彼百戰百勝」，投稿者若能了解國際期刊評審科技論文的要求，將有助於讓我們投出去能順利被接受進而刊登。一般說來，期刊評審分為：（1）匿名評審（anonymous review）；（2）親善式評審（friendly review）；（3）內部互審（internal review）。

國際期刊較多採用匿名評審，期刊編輯通常會選該投稿文章內參考文獻的作者作為評審，屬於同儕式評審 (peer review)；但較正規有水準期刊會挑選較具專業的專家與大師評審，不過，這些專家與大師由於太忙會轉給其博士生來進行初審，因此，本質上仍屬於同儕式評審。至於「親善式評審」則屬於某些 Communication 的期刊採用，例如：International Communication Heat and Mass Transfer 採用，評審較迅速且保留自己編排風格刊出。最後談到「內部互審」通常是校內學報或研討會採用，較不具公信力。

加州伯克來大學，Alan Mier [7] 在其發表的「如何評審科技論文」中明白指出論文評審的必要性理由係發現出論文中缺失如下：

1. 技術性鑽研方法與分析

2. 計算

3. 相關研究之遺漏

4. 困擾讀者之風格與文法

5. 專利或合法發行性

Alan Mier亦提及評審主要包括四個工作項目：

1. 審查之評審表

2. 附加評議

3. 原創性文章

4. 給編輯之說明信

至於附加的評議，應包括有利與不利兩方面意見。此點給編輯對某些關鍵性文章，做最後決定取捨的參考。基本上評審的主要評議係針對文章中假設、探究方法、分析、結果與討論、結論，以及參考文獻的適宜性評比；評審者儘可能作建設性改善的建議。另外，次要的評議係針對圖、表、語法與風格的建議。學者普遍認為，合理的結構是構成好文章之第一要素。

另外評審者要按照期刊規定的篇幅與參考文獻表現方式，建議作者做修改與刪除的動作。同時也要檢查所審文章的結論，是否直接由文章本體所綜合得到，並未再另行加入新的論點？最後仍要檢查在其所列參考文獻中，是否刻意遺漏某些已出版的重要文獻？

最後評審者提供總結建議給編輯，通常分成四種結果：

1. 以保持原文風貌刊出（publish as is）

2. 必須經過修正才可刊出（revise）

3. 建議修改成短篇論文再刊出（shorten as technical notes）

4. 拒絕刊出 (reject)

然後編輯再綜合兩個或以上的評審者意見，做最後裁決並寄回給作者。

根據一般學者的投稿經驗，有創新的、好的文章通常審查較久；相對的，較無創新、普通的文章審查時間會較短，除非遇到被不經意或太忙的評審拖延。因此，一段時間超過四個月，即可追查審查狀況。

總之，評審論文是件榮譽與回饋的工作，也搶先機先讀為快，有時也可因此得到一些研究的靈感；不過有一點要注意的，就是若遇到不適合我們的論文題目（專長不完全相符），也應該早一點退回編輯，這樣其實沒用什麼不好意思的；也可建議其他學者當評審者給編輯參考。

另外，在此也整理史丹佛大學的John Outsterhout's [8] 關於評審科技論文的看法如下：

一、評審目的

1. 協助導引期刊委員評選文章。

2. 幫助作者修正投稿的文章使可刊出，讓其了解被拒絕原因，或者讓作者了解如何改善進一步的研究與未來的計畫。

二、發行點 (Issues)

1. 是否提升研究領域？

2. 是否提出新見解？

3. 是否提出學理的證明證據？

4. 是否為實驗證實？

5. 是否可引起研討會討論？

6. 是否具可讀性？

7. 是否關係到更寬廣的研究領域？

☆ 讀者心得增補筆記欄 ☆

三、評價點

1. 待審文章嘗試探討什麼？

2. 待審文章具有潛力的貢獻是什麼？

3. 簡短歸納待審文章的優點與弱點是什麼？

4. 動機是否列出與使用方法是否正確？

5. 是否清楚不含混的陳述出文章？

6. 是否說明文章中觀念為何重要？

7. 文法是否正確？

   綜合上述作最後接受／修正／拒絕的決定！

☆ 讀者心得增補筆記欄 ☆

附錄四

科技論文之翻譯心得分享整理

1. 「主要子句（最後以時間名詞結束），when + ……」將 when 譯為「那時」或「當時」

……的學理開始於二十世紀，那時先鋒研究大師 Nusselt 開始鑽研……

The theory on... dated from the 20th century, when the pioneer researcher, Nusselt started to conduct...

2. 「主要子句，while + ……」while連接兩個對等子句時，將 while譯為「……，而……」

銅容易傳導熱而橡膠則不易

Copper conducts heat easily, while rubber will not.

3. As 引導從屬子句，主要子句

（1）若從屬子句主詞不同於主要子句的主詞，將as譯為「當時……（或隨著……），……」。

Y increases as X approaches... ；Y 隨著 X接近……而增加。

或譯為「當 X 接近……時，Y跟著增加」

As X increases, so does Y ；譯為「當 X 增加時，Y 也一樣增加」。

（2）「Just as 從屬子句，主要子句」將Just as「正像（如同）……；……也一樣（亦）……」。

正像質量守恆爲流體力學基礎；能量守恆亦爲熱力學基礎。

Just as the law of conservation of mass is the basis of fluid mechanics,

the law of conservation of energy is the basis of thermodynamics.

（3） 「主要子句 as 引導從屬子句」，當兩個子句相同時常省略主

詞，譯爲「……，這一點（主要子句主詞）……」。

冰融化時體積收縮，此點特性顯示在圖1。

Ice contracts slightly in volume when it melts, as (is) shown in Fig. 1

4. 不定詞：to＋V的翻譯如下

（1） 「To＋V……，主要子句」，譯爲「爲了……；」

爲了瞭解本過程是否遵守熱力學第二定律，我們必須檢查總熵值

變化是否不小於零。

To see why this process obeys the second law of thermodynamics, we

must check the net change in the total entropy is not less than zero.

（2） S＋V＋to＋V，置於句尾，譯爲「以便……」「來……」

「要……」

我們必須檢查總熵值變化來瞭解本過程是否遵守熱力學第二定

律。

We must check the net change in the total entropy to see if this process

obeys the second law of thermodynamics.

5. 祈使句，and 句子

（1） 譯爲「（若）……，就……」

練習此科技英文寫作，就可改善你的寫作風格。

Practice this technical English writing, and you will improve your writing style.

（2） 「祈使句，或（else、otherwise）句子」譯爲「……否則……」或「如果不……，就（會）……」

停止超速，否則被罰。

Stop speeding, or you will be fined.

6. 「主要子句 so that＋……」，譯爲「……以致於……」或「……因而……」或「……使得（以便）……」若 so that＋否定子句，譯爲「以免（免得）……」

金屬電線的電阻足夠低，以至於少許電位差即可使電流通過。

The resistance of the metal wire is low enough so that small potential difference may send the electric current flowing through it.

7. 「主要子句 such that＋……」，譯爲「……使得……」或「……因此……」

爆炸威力大到因此將所有窗戶震破。

The force of the explosion was such that all the windows were broken.

8. Now譯爲「此刻……」或「目前……」

此刻（目前）爲眞但是你並不期待它永遠爲眞。

It is true now but you do not expect it to be permanent.

置於句首「Now,...「譯爲「那麼……」或「於是……」

那麼，你認爲那是什麼？

Now, what do you think it was？

9.「Thus,... 」=「In this way,... 」譯爲「因此……」或「因而……」或

「這樣……」或「於是……」

我的老闆雇一位能幹的秘書。因此（於是），他能有效率的工作。

My boss employed a capable secretary. Thus, he was able to do his work

efficiently.

這樣，可以含 X 的項式來定義D。

In this way, D is defined in terms of X.

10.「…… for＋名詞」譯爲「爲……」或「適於名詞的……」或「……名

詞的……」

（1）創造性思考的能力：capacity for original thought.

（2）適於電燈泡的材料：the right material for the electric light balls.

（3）這些運算適合列並不適合行：These operations are for rows, not for

columns.

（4）新產品的需求：the demand for new products.

（5）名詞的符號：the symbol for名詞

（6）我們由基本定理獲得齊次系統的下列結果。

For the homogeneous system we obtain from the Fundamental Theorem the following results.

◎ 句型分析：此為倒裝句，原來句子為

We obtain from the Fundamental Theorem the following results for the homogeneous system.

10.「……名詞 for＋動名詞」，譯為「用來做什麼的名詞」

（1）用來轉換熱成功的設備：a device for converting heat into work.

（2）用來解決……問題的方法：a method for solving the problem of...

（3）做研究計劃的能力：an ability for doing the research project.

11.「……介係詞片語＋名詞……」

（1）對名詞的：with respect to名詞

例如：對時間的導數（微分）：the derivative with respect to time

（2）對應於名詞的：corresponding to名詞

例如：對應於x值的y範圍：a range of y corresponding to x

（3）以x表示的y：y in terms of x

例如：超過0.8的係數：coefficient in excess of 0.8

（4）最大值到10的參數B：parameter B up to 10

例如：由摩擦引起的熵增生：entropy generation due to friction

12.「From... it follows that... 」譯爲「由……可推知」

從定義可推知我們可對任意列或行展開一行列式。

From the definition it follows that we may expand a determinant by any row or column.

☆ 讀者心得增補筆記欄 ☆

☆ 讀者心得增補筆記欄 ☆

附錄五

科技論文常用名、
動詞搭配

Account：評價、考慮

1. V+N： take... of = take into... 對……加以考慮

2. V+Prep.+N： ... for... 說明

   turn... to good account 善加利用

3. Adj.+N： much... 重要

   no... 不重要

   little... 輕視

   further... 進一步評價、考慮

   take further account of... take (=make) much /little/no account of

   重／輕／忽視

◎ 注意：Account 當動詞亦為「評價；考慮」account for sth. 說明某事理由。

Agreement：同意；一致

1. V+N： arrive at/come to/reach on... 達成協議（一致）

   break on... 違反協定

   make (conclude) an... on 簽訂……的協定

2. Prep+N： to be (show) in... 表示同意、……一致

Attention：注意

1. V+N： attract/catch/capture/draw/get... 吸引……的注意

   focus one's... on/devote one's... to 專注於

   direct/turn one's... to 將注意力轉向於

2. Adj.+N： close...　密切注意

a lot of (= much) attention　許多注意

pay much/little/no attention to　相當／稍微／不注意

Attitude：態度、心態

1. V+N： adopt/assume/take an... to (= toward)　對……採取……的態度

2. Adj.+N： a positive...　積極態度

a negative...　消極態度

a resolute...　堅決態度

a hands-off...　袖手旁觀的態度

a liberal...　寬宏的態度。

Arrangement：安排

1. V+N： arrive at/come to/conclude an...　達成安排

2. Adj.+N： advance...　預先安排

flower...　插花

Analysis：分析

1. V+N： elude　無從分析

make an　做分析

2. Adj.+N： A further　進一步分析

in-depth　深度分析

careful/painstaking/thorough　徹底、仔細分析

3. Prep. + N： Upon/On　經分析後

Action：行動

1. V+N： bring/take... against sb. for sth.　因某事對某人採取行動

2. Adj.+N： concerted/united...　一致的行動

hasty/rash...　草率的行動

Address：演說

1. V+N： deliver/give/make an...　演說＝address

2. Adj.+N： a(n) eloquent/moving/stirring...　動人的演說

Acquaintance：認識

1. V+N： gain/have... with　熟悉

make the... of sb.　認識某人

2. Adj.+N： a casual/nodding...　點頭（泛泛）之交

some/a slight...　略知

an intimate...　摯友

Accommodation：設備或容納空間

1. V+N： afford/furnish/give good... s　提供良好（住宿）設備

come to/reach / work out an...　達成協議（可容納空間）

2. Adj.+N： deluxe/capital... s　豪華／上等設備

Achievement vs. A0chieve：成就v s. 完成

1. V+N： achieve success　獲得成功

achieve one's goal　達成某人目標

2. Adj.+N： academic achievement　學術成就

outstanding achievement　傑出成就

Admiration vs. Admire：讚賞

1. V+N： command/win...　贏得讚賞

express/feel... for sb.= admire for sb.　讚賞某人

2. Adj.+N： great...　非常讚賞

Attempt：嘗試

1. V+N： make an... /at +Ving/to+V　嘗試去做什麼

= attempt + N；attempt an escape　企圖逃走

attempt a difficult problem　試圖解決難題

Assignment：分配、指定工作

1. V+N： allot...　分配任務

　　　　 carry out/ fulfill an...　完成任務

　　　　 hand in...　交作業

2. Adj.+N： a difficult/rough/tough...　艱鉅任務

Article：物件、文章

1. V+N： clip an... from　自……剪下一篇文章

　　　　 contribute an... to　投稿至……。

2. Adj.+N： a feature...　特寫

　　　　 a leading...　社論

　　　　 a solid...　有內容之文章

Authority：權威

1. V+N： cite/invoke an...　引經據典

　　　　 establish...　建立權威

　　　　 have/posses... over　對……有權限

2. Adj.+N： absolute/complete/full/supreme...　絕對權威

　　　　 parental...　父母權威

　　　　 the proper... ies/the... ies concerned　有關當局

Backache：背痛

1. V+N： have (a)...　背痛。

2. Adj.+N： (a) chronic...　慢性背痛

(a) nagging...　惱人的背痛

(a)persistent...　久背痛

Baggage (luggage)：行李

1. V+N： book /check one's... through to...　把行李託運到……

claim one's...　認領行李

2. Adj.+N： heavy...　笨重行李

light...　輕便行李

Ballet：芭蕾舞

1. V+N： attend a...　去觀賞芭蕾舞

dance a...　跳芭蕾舞

perform a...　表演芭蕾舞

stage a...　演出芭蕾舞

2. Adj.+N： classical...　古典芭蕾舞

folk...　民族芭蕾舞；

(a)water...　水上芭蕾舞

Bandage：繃帶

1.V+N：　　　　　apply / put on a...　用繃帶包紮

　　　　　　　　　remove a...　拿掉繃帶。

Bank：銀行

1. V+N：　　　　　borrow money from a...　向銀行貸款

　　　　　　　　　carry on /conduct /direct /manage a...　經營銀行

　　　　　　　　　deposit / lodge /put money in a...　在銀行存款

　　　　　　　　　draw / withdraw money from a...　向銀行提款

2. N+V：　　　　　A... collapses / fails.　銀行倒閉

Bar：酒吧、酒吧

1. V+N：　　　　　be admitted / called to the...　獲准擔任律師

　　　　　　　　　manage / operate / run a...　經營酒吧

2. Adj.+N：　　　　a horizontal...　單槓

　　　　　　　　　parallel... s　雙槓

Barrier：障礙

1. V+N：　　　　　break down / demolish a...　拆毀障礙物

　　　　　　　　　build / erect / place / put (up) / set up a...　設置障礙

　　　　　　　　　overcome a...　克服障礙

　　remove a...　清除障礙

2. Adj.+N： a cultural... 文化障礙

a language... （異邦之間的）語言障礙

a racial... 種族障礙

Basket：籃

1. V+N： make / score / shoot / sink a... （籃球）投進得分

miss the... 投籃未中

shoot at the... 投籃

2. Adj.+N： a lunch... 午餐籃

a picnic... 野餐籃

a shopping... 購物籃

a waste-paper... 廢紙簍

Basis ：基礎

1. V+N： establish / lay the... of [for]... 建立……的基礎

2. 介+名： on a... / on the... of 以……為基礎

Battery ：電池

1. V+N： change a... 換電池

charge a... 給電池充電

recharge a... 給電池再充電。

2. N+V： The... has run down.　電池的電用完了

The... is dead.　電池發不動了

Battle：作戰

1. V+N： do... with　與…作戰

fight / wage a...　作戰

gain / win a...　戰勝

join...　參戰

lose a...　戰敗

Bayonet：刺刀

1. V+N： Fix... s!　（口令）上刺刀！

Thrust a... into sb.'s body　用刺刀刺入某人身體

Beard：鬍鬚

1. V+N： cultivate / grow / wear a...　留鬍鬚

shave off one's...　剃鬍鬚

stoke one's...　捋鬍子

trim one's...　修鬍鬚

2. Adj.+N： a busy / heavy / thick...　濃密的鬍鬚

a light / sparse...　稀疏的鬍鬚

Beautify：美化

1. V+N： ... city streets　美化街道

... our environment　美化我們的環境

... the face　美容

... life by art　以藝術美化人生

Bed：床

1. V+N： be confined to / keep / take / to one's bed　臥病在床

climb into...　爬上床

get into / go to...　上床

get out of...　起床

jump out of...　跳下床

make a [one's , (the)] bed　鋪床

Beauty ：美

1. V+N： cultivate one's...　陶冶某人的美感

hold / stage a...　舉行選美比賽

enter a...　參加選美比賽

2. Adj.+N： Beauty charms sb.　美迷住某人

Beauty contest　選美比賽

Beg：討；請

1. V+Adv.：　　　... humbly　低聲下氣的乞討（求）

2. V+N：　　　　... food　乞討食物

　　　　　　　　　... your forgiveness　請原諒

　　　　　　　　　... your pardon　對不起

　　　　　　　　　... your permission　請你准許

Behave：行為

1. V+Adv.：　　　... admirably　行為可佩

　　　　　　　　　... badly　行為不良

　　　　　　　　　... bravely　行為勇敢

2. V+Prep.：　　　... like / as a gentleman　舉止像紳士

Behavior：行為

1. V+N：　　　　exhibit strange...　行為怪異

2. Adj.+N：　　　admirable...　令人欽佩的行為

　　　　　　　　　barbaric...　野蠻行為

　　　　　　　　　cruel...　殘忍的行為

　　　　　　　　　prudent...　謹慎的行為

　　　　　　　　　rude...　粗魯的行為

Belief：相信

1. V+N： express / hold a... that 相信

give up one's... that 放棄信念

Bell：鈴聲

1. V+N： answer the... 應門鈴

ring / sound a... 按鈴

2. Adj.+N： an alarm... 警鈴

an electric... 電鈴

Celt：帶子

1. V+N： buckle the... 扣上帶子

fasten one's... 綁緊帶子

loosen one's... 放鬆帶子

2. Adj.+N： a safty/seat... 安全帶

a conveyor... 輸送帶

Belt：打賭

1. V+N： accept/take a... 同意打賭

lose a... 輸掉打賭

make a... on　打賭

win a...　賭贏。

Bias：偏見

1. V+N：　　　demonstrate/display/exhibit/show... (against/toward)　對…有偏

見

root out...　　根除偏見

2. Adj.+N：　　a deep-rooted... 根深柢固偏見

racial...　　種族偏見

religious...　　宗教偏見

Bill：議案

1. V+N：　　　draft a...

foot / pay a...　草擬議案

introduce a...　提出議案

pass a...　通過議案

veto a...　否決議案

2. Adj.+N：　　A... falls due / matures.　帳單到期

Bite：咬

1. V+N：   grab / have a...　匆匆吃下

　　　　　　　　take a... out of the apple　咬下一口蘋果

Blame：責備

1. V+N：   ascribe / assign / attribute the... to sb　歸因於某人

　　　　　　　　lay / place / put the... on sb　責備某人

Bleeding：流血

1. V+N：   staunch / stop the...　止血

2. Adj.+N：   heavy / profuse...　大量流血

Blood：血

1. V+N：   donate...　捐血

　　　　　　　　lose...　輸血

　　　　　　　　take sb's... pressure　量血腥

　　　　　　　　type sb's...　驗血型

Bloom：開花

1. V+N：   be in...　花盛開

　　　　　　　　come into...　開花

Boycott：抵制；杯葛

1. V+N： impose a... on imports　杯葛進口貨

institute/launch a...　發起抵制

lift a... of　解除……杯葛

Breeze：微風

1. V+N： A... blows　微風吹起

A... comes up　微風起

Broadcast：廣播

1. V+N： ... a concert (the news)　音樂（新聞）廣播

2. Adj.+N： a live...　現場廣播

nationwide...　全國廣播

Blow：泡泡

1. V+N： blow... s　吹泡泡

burst a...　弄泡泡

prick/punch a...　刺破泡泡

2. Adj.+N： air... s　氣泡

soap... s　肥皂泡泡

Budget：預算

1. V+N：   add to / enlarge / increase...   增加預算

                     balance a...   平衡預算

                     cut down / reduce...   減少預算

                     exceed a...   超過預算

Building：建築

1. V+N：   build / erect / put up a...   起造建築

                     demolish / raze / tear down...   拆掉建築

                     renovate...   修理建築

2. Adj.+N：   a big / large...   大建築

                     a dilapidated / troubledown...   破舊建築

Call：電話、訪問

1. V+N：   answer / heed / respond to a...   回應某一召喚

                     have / receive a...   接到電話

                     make / pay a... on sb.   拜訪某人

                     put a... through   接通電話

                     return sb.'s...   回訪某人

2. Adj.+N：   a collect...　由受話人付費的電話

　　　　　　　　a dial-direct...　直撥電話

　　　　　　　　a long-distance / toll...　長途電話

　　　　　　　　a person-to-person...　叫人電話

　　　　　　　　a station–to-station...　叫號電話

Camp：營帳

1. V+N：   break / stride a...　拔營

　　　　　　　make / pitch /set up a...　紮營

2. Adj.+N：   a concentration...　集中營

　　　　　　　　a refugee...　難民營

　　　　　　　　a summer...　夏令營

Campaign：選舉活動

1. V+N：   carry on / wage a...　發起某運動

2. Adj.+N：   an active / vigorous...　積極有力的運動

　　　　　　　　a "don't buy" ...　拒購運動

　　　　　　　　a nationwide...　全國性的運動

　　　　　　　　a whirlwind...　旋風式的運動

Capacity：容量、才能

1. V+N： develop the reasoning... ies　培養推理能力

be filled to...　滿座

2. Adj.+N： a great... for music　音樂才能很高

operate at full / peak...　全力運轉

mental...　智力

seating...　座位容納量

Capital：資本

1. V+N： invest / put up...　投入資金

make... of　利用

raise...　籌措資金

redeem a... invested　收回投資

sink a... in...　投資於⋯⋯

withdraw...　撤資。

2. Adj.+N： circulating / floating...　流動資本

fixed...　固定資本

foreign...　外資

idle / unemployed...　閒置資本

working...　週轉資金

Care：關懷、照料、小心

1. V+N：　　　　exercise / take...　當心注意

2. Adj.+N：　　　great / meticulous...　極度小心

intensive... units　加護病房

medical...　醫療

Career：生涯

1. V+N：　　　　enter on a business...　投入企業界

pursue a... in...　從事……方面的行業

wreck a...　斷送前途

2. Adj.+N：　　　a brilliant...　輝煌的事業生涯

one's college...　大學生活

Case：案件、情況

1. V+N：　　　　argue/ plead a...　為某案辯護

dismiss / throw out a...　不受理某案件

drop a...　撤回訴訟

investigate / work on a...　調查某案件

2. Adj.+N：　　　an acute...　急性病

a chronic...　慢性病

a civil...　民事案件

a criminal...　刑事案件

Cash：現金

1. V+N：　　　pay...　付現

run out of...　現金用罄

2. Adj.+N：　　cold / hard...　硬幣

ready...　現款

spare...　餘款

Casualties：傷亡

1. V+N：　　　cause...　造成傷亡

incur / suffer...　遭受傷亡

2. Adj.+N：　　heavy / serious...　嚴重傷亡

slight...　輕微傷亡

traffic...　交通傷亡

Ceiling：限度

1. V+N：　　　abolish / lift a...　解除上限

lowe a...　降低限度

place / set a... ；raise a...　設定限度

Celebration：慶祝

1. V+N： hold a... 舉行慶祝

   sponsor a... 主辦慶祝

2. Adj.+N： the Double Tenth... 雙十國慶。

Censorship：檢查

1. V+N： abolish/lift... 廢除檢查

   impose... 加以檢查

   exercise... 實施檢查

2. Adj.+N： film... 影片檢查

   press... 新聞檢查

   rigid/strict... 嚴格檢查

Ceremony：儀式

1. V+N： conduct / hold / perform a... 舉行儀式

2. Adj.+N： an awarding... 頒獎典禮

   a closing... 閉幕典禮

   an opening... 開幕典禮

Challenge：挑戰

1. V+N： accept / repond to / take up a...　接受挑戰

issue/send a...　下挑戰

Chance：機會

1. V+N： have / stand a... of success　有成功希望

let a... slip by　錯失機會

2. Adj.+N： a poor / slight / slim...　機會很小

Change：改變

1. V+N： bring about / effect / make a...　造成改變

get / take one's...　找零錢

2. Adj.+N： a drastic...　徹底改變

a marked...　顯著改變

a personnel...　人事變動

Charge：指控

1. V+N： bring / level / make a...　指控

dismiss / throw up a...　不受理指控

deny/refuse...　否認指控

drop / retract / withdraw a...　撤銷指控

2. Adj.+N： a baseless / fabricated...　不實指控

Charity：慈悲、慈愛

1. V+N： ask for / beg for...　請求布施

bestow... on / dispense... to　布施

Charm：魅力

1. V+N： exude...　散發魅力

turn on / use one's...　運用魅力

Check：支票

1. V+N： cash a...　以支票兌現款

draw / issue / make out / write (out) a...　開支票

endorse a...　在支票上背書

stop payment of a...　支票止付

2. Adj.+N： a bad / dishonored / rubber...　空頭支票

a blank...　空白支票

Checkup：檢查

1. V+N： do / give a...　檢查

have a　作檢查

2. Adj.+N： an annual... 年度檢查

a regular... 定期檢查

Cheer：歡呼

1. V+N： acknowledge the... s 答謝喝采

draw a... 博得歡呼

enjoy / make good... 吃喝作樂

give/shout a... 歡呼

2. Adj.+N： Christmas... 聖誕節佳餚

good... 振作起來

a loud/rousing... 大聲歡呼

Circle：圓、圈圈

1. V+N： describe/draw a... 畫圓圈

square a... 做不可能的事

2. Adj.+N： acdemic... s 學術界

business... s 工商界

the upper... s 上流社會

a vicious... 惡性循環

Circulation：發行

1. V+N： have a large / wide...　大的發行量

limited / small...　小發行量

Circumstances：情況、週遭

1. Adj.+N： in adverse / trying...　逆境

in favorable...　順境

Claim：要求、主張

1. V+N： enter / file / make / put in a...　提出主張

give up / renounce / waive a...　放棄要求

lay... to　宣稱

Clause：條款

1. V+N： alter a...　變更條款

erase a...　刪除條款

violate a...　違反條款

waive a...　放棄條款

2. Adj.+N： an additional...　附加條款

a contract...　合約條款

a secret...　秘密條款

Clue：線索

1. V+N： discover / find a...　發現線索

furnish / provide a...　提供線索

Comfort：安慰

1. V+N： bring / give / provide...　帶來安慰

derive... from　獲得安慰

find / seek / take... in　尋求安慰

2. Adj.+N： cold / little...　起不了作用的安慰

plain / simple... s　簡便生活舒適用品

Comment：評論

1. V+N： arouse/evoke/excite...　引起評論

2. Adj. +N： appropriate / fitting...　適當的評論

favorable...　有利的評論

critical / scathing / unfavorable...　苛刻、不利的評論

Compassion：同情

1. V+N： arouse... 引起同情

demonstrate / display / show... 表示同情

Competition：競爭

1. V+N： bitter / fierce / keen / strong... 競爭

cutthroat / unfair / unscrupulous 惡性、不正當競爭

free / unflettered... 自由競爭

healthy... 良性競爭

Complaint：抱怨

1. V+N： bring / file / lodge / make a... 提出抱怨

disregard / ignore... 不理會抱怨

2. Adj. +N： a bitter / loud... 極力抱怨

Compliment：恭維

1. V+N： lavish / shower... on 極力恭維

Composition：作文、作曲

1. V+N： do / write a... 寫作

perform a... 演奏曲子

Compromise：妥協

1. V+N：   reach / work out a...   達成妥協

Concern：關切

1. V+N：   arouse / cause / give...   引起關切

                     express / voice...   表達關切

2. Adj.+N：   grave / serious...   嚴重關切

                     particular...   特別關切

                     primary...   主要關切

Concession：退讓

1. V+N：   grant / make a...   讓步

Conclusion：結論

1. V+N：   arrive at / come to / draw / reach a...   達成結論

                     make a...   下結論

2. Adj. +N：   a hasty / rash...   草率結論

                     a rational/reasonable... 合理結論

Condition：條件

1. V+N：　　　　　better / ameliorate the... s of　改善……的條件

　　　　　　　　　　fufill / meet / satify a...　切合……條件

　　　　　　　　　　impose / set a...　設定……條件

2. Adj. +N：　　　　an essential...　重要條件

　　　　　　　　　　a critical...　關鍵條件

Conduct：行為、指導、處理

1. Adj.+N：　　　　courageous　勇敢行為

　　　　　　　　　　foolish / silly...　愚蠢行為

　　　　　　　　　　odd...　怪異行為

　　　　　　　　　　shameful...　可恥行為

Confidence：信心

1. V+N：　　　　　gain / win sb.'s...　取得某人信任

　　　　　　　　　　have / place / put... in　對... 有信心

　　　　　　　　　　lose... in　失去信心

　　　　　　　　　　shake sb.'s...　動搖信心

2. Adj. +N：　　　　absolute / perfect... in　完全信心

Conflict：衝突

1. V+N：　　　　prevent a...　避免衝突

provoke a...　引起衝突

resolve a...　解決衝突

Confusion：困惑

1. V+N：　　　　cause...　造成困惑

clear up...　釐清困惑

throw into...　陷入困惑

2. Adj. +N：　　complete / ulter...　困惑至極

Congratulations：恭喜

1. V+N：　　　　cable / telegraph one's... to　致電道賀

extend / offer one's... to　向……道賀。

2. Adj. +N：　　hearty / sincere / warm...　衷心道賀。

Connection：關聯

1. V+N：　　　　establish/make a...　建立關係

break / sever a...　斷絕關係

2. Adj. +N：　　a close / an intimate...　密切關係

a loose / tenuous...　疏遠關係

Conscience：良心

1. V+N：   appeal to...　訴諸良心

                      arous one's...　使良心發現

                      ease one's...　使安心

2. Adj. +N：   have a clean / clear / good...　問心無愧

                      have a bad / guilty...　內心不安

Consciousness：意識

1. V+N：   lose...　失去知覺

                      regain...　恢復知覺

2. Adj. +N：   class...　階級意識

                      intense...　強烈意識

Consequence：後果

1. V +N：   accept / bear the...　承受後果

2. Adj. +N：   far-reaching...　影響深遠後果

                      grave / serious...　嚴重後果

Constitution：憲法

1. V +N：   abrogate a...　廢除憲法

                      amend / revise...　修改憲法

draw up / frame / write a... 起草憲法

estabilsh... 建立憲法

Preserve a... 維護憲法

violate a... 違反憲法

Contact：接觸、連綴

1. V +N： break off... 斷絕交往

come in / into... with 與……接觸

establish / make... with 開始接觸

Contempt：鄙視、完全不理

1. V +N： show... for 鄙視

throw... on 侮辱

Contract：合約

1. V +N： breach / break / violate a... 違約

cancel... 取消合約

carry out / execute a... 執行合約

make / enter into a... 簽約

Contrast：對比

1. V +N： form / offer / present a... to　與……形成對比

2. Adj. +N： a glaring / harsh/sharp / startling / striking...　顯著對比

Contribution：貢獻

1. V +N： a brilliant / a notable / an outstanding / a remarkable...　傑出貢獻。

Controversy：爭論

1. V +N： arouse / cause / fuel / provoke / stir up...　引起爭論

enter into / have / hold a... with　與……爭論

Settle a...　解決爭論

terminate a...　終止爭論

2. Adj.+N： a bitter / furious / heated / hot...　激烈爭論

a labor-management...　勞資糾紛

Conviction：信念

1. Adj.+N： previous... s　前科

solid / strong / unshaken...　堅定信念

Cooperation：合作

1. V +N：   lend active... to   給予……積極合作

                    promote... among   促進……之間合作

2. Adj.+N：   close...   密切合作

                    mutual...   互相合作

Corner：角落

1. V+N：   cut... s   抄近路

                    establish / make a... in   囤積、壟斷

2. Adj.+N：   a blind...   死角

                    the four... s of the globe   全球各地

Correspondence：通信、相符、一致

1. V+N：   break off...   斷絕書信連繫

                    carry on / conduct a...   進行書信往來

2. Adj.+N：   business...   商業書信

Cost：成本、花費

1. V+N：   bear a...   負擔費用

                    cut / reduce... s   降低費用

                    estimate a...   預估費用

2. Adj.+N： direct... s　直接成本

fixed... s　固定成本

overhead... s　經常性費用

Counsel：忠告

1. V+N： give / offer / provide...　給予忠告

hold / take... with sb.　聽某人忠告

2. Adj.+N： a legal...　法律顧問

a wise...　明智的勸告

Courage：勇氣

1. V+N： get up / muster / screw up / summon up...　鼓起勇氣

lose...　喪失勇氣

2. Adj.+N： dauntless / indomitable...　不屈不橈的勇氣

moral...　道德勇氣

Craving：渴望

1. V+N： feel / have a... for　渴望

satisfy one's...　滿足某人的渴望

2. Adj.+N： a powerful / strong...　強烈的欲望

Date：日期

1. V+N：

break / cut a...　爽約

fix / set　a...　定日期

go out on / have a... with　與……約會

keep a...　守約

make a... with　與……定約。

2. Adj.+N：

a closing...　截止日期

a definite...　確切日期

at an early...　近日

Dabble：涉獵、涉足

1. V+介：

... at painting　（業餘）涉獵繪畫

... in politics　玩政治

... in stocks / play the stock market　玩股票

Damages：損害、賠償費

1. V+N：

clain...　要求賠償費

pay...　負賠償費

receive...　收到賠償費

sue for...　控告要求賠償費

2. V+N： cause / do... to　使……受到損害

inflict... on　對…施加傷害

suffer / sustain...　受到損害

work...　造成損失

Deadline：最後期限

1. V+N： establish / set a...　確定最後期限

Extend a...　延後限期

meet a...　遵守限期

miss a...　未能在限期前完成

Deal ：交易

1. V+N： close / do / make / strike / wrap up a... with...　與……達成交易。

2. Adj+N： a barter...　以貨易貨

Big... !　大驚小怪

a package...　整批交易

a rough...　不公平的待遇

Death：死亡

1. V+N：　　　　face...　面對死亡

feign...　裝死

Debate：辯論會

1. V+N：　　　　conduct / have / hold a...　舉行辯論會

Debt：債

1. V+N：　　　　clear (off) / clear up / discharge / extinguish / pay off one's...　還

清債務；

Contract / get into / incur / run up a...　負債

pay one's...　還債

repudiate a...　賴債

Deck：甲板、底板

1. V+N：　　　　cut a...　切牌，分牌

shuffle a...　洗牌

stack a...　做牌（洗牌時作弊）

Declaration：宣告

1. V+N：　　　　issue / make a...　宣言、宣布

2. Adj+N：   customs...　報關

    a solemn...　鄭重宣布

Decline：衰減

1. Adj+N：   a gradual...　逐漸式微

    a sharp...　急遽下降或衰退

    a steady...　持續衰微

Decree：命令

1. V+N：   enact a...　制定法令

    issue a...　發布命令

    rescind / revoke a...　廢除法令

Dedication：獻身

1. V+N：   demonstrate / display... to　獻身於……

Deed：權狀、行為、功業

1. Adj+N：   a title...　不動產權狀、地契

2. V+N：   transfer a title...　移轉不動產權狀

Defect：缺點

1. V+N：　　　　correct a...　改正缺點

2. Adj+N：　　　a birth...　天生的缺陷

　　　　　　　　a hearing...　聽力障礙

　　　　　　　　a physical...　生理缺陷

　　　　　　　　a speech...　言語缺陷

Defense / defence：防衛

1. V+N：　　　　conduct / make a... against　防禦、防衛

　　　　　　　　strengthen the... s　加強防禦

2. Adj+N：　　　civil...　民防

　　　　　　　　a man-to-man...　（運動）緊迫盯人戰術

　　　　　　　　military...　軍防

　　　　　　　　national...　國防

Delight：喜悅

1. V+N：　　　　feel / take... in　樂於……

　　　　　　　　give... to　使……喜悅

2. Adj+N：　　　great / intense / sheer...　非常愉快

Delivery：投遞

1. Adj+N： aerial...　空投

a difficult...　（產婦）難產

an easy...　（產婦）順產

express / specia l...　（郵件）快遞

a natural...　自然分娩

a painless...　無痛分娩

Demand：需求

1. V+N： drop a...　放棄要求（權）

give in to a...　舉行示範表演

make / stage a...　舉行示威運動

Denounce：譴責

1. V+Adv： ... hotly / vehemently / vigorously / violently　強烈譴責

... sternly　嚴厲譴責

Denunciation：譴責

1. V+N： issue / make a　公然譴責

Deny：否認

1. V+Adv： ... categorically / flatly　斷然否認

... fervently / vehemently　強烈否認

Deposit：訂金、存款

1. V+N： leave / make a... on a car　為購車付訂金

make a... in a bank　把錢存進銀行

2. Adj+N： a current / demand...　活到存款

a fixed / time...　定期存款

3. N+PERP： ... in foreign currency　外幣存款

a... of ＄250　兩百五十元訂金

pay a on the house　付房子訂金

Depth：深度

1. V+N： lack...　缺乏深度、膚淺

2. Prep+N： beyond / out of one's...　深到沒頂的地方、無法理解

five feet in...　五呎深

Description：描述

1. V+N： baffle / beggar / defy...　無法形容

2. Adj+N： a broad...　大略的描述

a detailed / elaborate...　詳盡的描述

Destination：目的地

1. V+N：   arrive at / reach one's...   到達目的地

Detail：細節

1. V+N：   bring up / cite... s   引述細節

                 enter into / go into... (s)   詳述

                 fill in(the)... s   填上細節

                 furnish(the)... s   提供細節

                 give a full... of   詳述……

Determination：決心

1. V+N：   come to a...   下定決心

                 declare / show...   表示決心

2. Adj+N：   a(n) dogged / firm / iron / unflinching / unyielding...   堅定的決心。

Development：發展

1. V+N：   arrest / check / hamper / prevent the... of   阻礙……的發展

                 promote...   促進發展

Devote：奉獻

1. V+O+Perp： ... oneself completely / entirely to... 完全獻身於……

... one's life to... 貢獻於一生

... one's time to 奉獻時間做……。

Digestion：消化

1. V+N： aid / help... 幫助消化

disturb / impair / spoil / upset one's... 妨礙消化

promote... 促進消化

Dignity：尊嚴

1. V+N： hurt / impair the... 損害尊嚴

maintain one's... 保持尊嚴

possess... 具有威嚴

Dinner：晚餐

1. V+N： eat / have... 吃晚餐

hold a... 舉行晚宴

make / prepare... 作晚餐

Director：導演

1. Adj.+N：　　　　a company...　公司董事

　　　　　　　　　a film / screen...　電影導演

　　　　　　　　　a stage...　舞台導演

Disaster：災難

1. V+N：　　　　　cause / court / invite...　惹禍

　　　　　　　　　experience / meet / suffer (a)...　遭受災害

2. Adj+N：　　　　an air...　空難

　　　　　　　　　a national...　國難

Discipline：紀律

1. V+N：　　　　　crack down on violations of...　嚴厲處罰違紀

　　　　　　　　　establish...　建立紀律

Discount：折扣

1. V+N：　　　　　give / make 10%... on the list price　照定價打九折

　　　　　　　　　get a...　得到折扣

Discretion：慎重

1. V+N： exercise / show / use... in 謹慎做……

Discrimination：差別、歧視

1. V+N： practice... 歧視

lack... 缺乏辨識力

2. Adj+N： aesthetic... 審美力

race / racial... 種族歧視

sex... 性別歧視

3. N+Prep： ... against Asians 歧視亞洲人

4. V+N： resolve / settle a... 解決爭端

stir up a... about 激起……的爭論

5. V+N： cover / run / travel / walk a... of 30miles 跑（走）三十英里

keep a safe... between cars 車子保持安全距離

Disturbance：動亂、干擾

1. V+N： cause / create / make / raise a... 引起騷動

put down / quell a... 鎮壓動亂

2. Adj.+N： a digestive... 消化不良

a labor... 工潮

a political...　政治動亂

a school...　學潮

Draft：匯票

1. V+N：　　　honor a...　承兌（支付）匯票

2. Adj.+N：　　a bad...　假匯票

　　　　　　　a bank...　銀行匯票

　　　　　　　a sight...　即期匯票

　　　　　　　a time...　定期匯票。

Draft：草稿

1. V+N：　　　dodge / evade the...　逃避兵役

　　　　　　　make / prepare a...　起草稿

2. Adj.+N：　　a final...　定稿

　　　　　　　a polished...　潤飾稿

　　　　　　　a preliminary / rough...　初稿、草稿

Drill：練習

1. Adj.+N：　　a class...　課堂練習

　　　　　　　a fire...　消防演習

　　　　　　　a grammatical...　文法練習

a military...　軍事訓練

a pattern...　句型練習

Diagnosis：診斷

1. V+N：　　　confirm a...　證實某判斷

give / make a... (of)　診斷、分析

Diamond：鑽石

1. V+N：　　　cut a...　切割鑽石

grind / polish a...　琢磨鑽石

set a...　錶鑽石

Diary：日記

1. V+N：　　　keep a... 記日記

write a... 寫日記

2. Adj+N：　　a personal... 私人日記

a pocket...　袖珍日記本

a travel...　旅行日記

Diet：飲食、節食

1. V+N：　　　be on / follow / go on a...　照規定飲食

2. Adj+N：　　　　a liquid...　流體飲食

　　　　　　　　　a meatless...　素食

Difficulty、困難

1. V+N：　　　　cause / create / make... ties for...　給……帶來困難

　　　　　　　　　clear up / overcome / resolve / surmount a...　解決困難

　　　　　　　　　come across / encounter / run into... ties　遭遇困難

Duel：決鬥、抗爭

1.V+N.：　　　　challenge sb. to a...　向……挑戰決鬥

　　　　　　　　　fight / have a... with　與……決鬥

2. N+ V：　　　　A... took place.　發生決鬥

3. Adj.+N：　　　have a verbal... with　與……舌戰

Dump：傾倒

1. Adj.+N：　　　a garbage / rubbish / trash...　垃圾場

Duty：責任

1. V+N：　　　　assume / take on a...　承擔責任

　　　　　　　　　carry out / discharge a...　完成任務

do / perform one's...　盡職

escape / shirk one's...　逃避責任

2. Adj.+N：　　do one's filial...　盡孝道

a moral...　道德上的義務

perform... ies　執行公務

Dynasty：王朝

1. V+N：　　establish / found a...　創建王朝

overthrow a...　推翻王朝

Enthusiasm：熱心

1. V+N：　　arouse / kindle / stip up... for　引起對……的熱中

dampen sb.'s...　潑某人冷水

demonstrate / display / show...　表示熱心

2. Adj.+N：　　boundless / unbounded...　極度熱心

patriotic...　愛國熱情

wild...　狂熱

Entrance：入口

1. Adj.+N：　　a back / rear...　後門

a front / main...　前門

a side...　側門

Envy：羨慕

1. V+N：　　　　arouse / stir up...　引起羨慕

　　　　　　　　feel... at　對……感到羨慕

Epidemic：時疫

1. V+N：　　　　control an...　控制時疫

　　　　　　　　stamp out an...　撲滅時疫

　　　　　　　　trigger an...　引起時疫... 花粉熱

　　　　　　　　a high...　高燒

　　　　　　　　a mild / slight...　輕微發燒

　　　　　　　　stage...　舞台熱

Enemy：敵人

1. V+N：　　　　conquer / overcome an...　征服敵人

2. Adj.+N：　　avowed / bitter / mortal... ies　不共戴天的敵人

　　　　　　　　a hereditary...　宿敵

Energy：能量、精力

1. Adj.+N：　　devote one's... to sth.　致力於某事

　　　　　　　　dissipate one's... on sth.　浪費精力於某事

Engagement：契約

1. V+N：　　　　break an...　毀約

enter into an... with　與……訂約

fulfil an...　踐約

2. Adj.+N：　　　a fierce...　激戰

a naval...　海上交戰

a previous / prior...　先前之約

Engine：引擎

1. V+N：　　　　crank / start an...　發動引擎

cut / kill turn off an...　關閉引擎

warm up an...　預熱引擎

2. N+ V：　　　　An... breaks down.　引擎出毛病

Eclipse：蝕

1. Adj.+N：　　　an annular...　環蝕

a full / total...　全蝕

a lunar...　月蝕

a partial...　偏蝕

a solar...　日蝕

Edition：成本

1. Adj.+N： an abridged... 節本

a deluxe... 豪華版

a hardback / hardbound / hardcover... 精裝本

a paperback... 平裝本

a pirated... 盜印版

a pocket... 袖珍版

a popular... 普及版

a revised... 修訂版

Education：教育

1. Adj.+N： adult... 成人教育

a college / university... 大學教育

elementary / primary... 小學教育

higher... 高等教育

liberal... 通才教育

secondary... 中等教育

Effect：效應

1. V+N： have / produce an... on 對……發生影響（效果）

heighten an... 提高效果

2. Adj.+N： an adverse...　不利的影響

a dramatic...　相當大的影響

a far-reaching...　深遠的影響

a marginal...　影響有限

Effort：努力

1. V+N： exert / make an...　盡力

spare no...　不遺餘力

redouble one's...　加倍努力

2. Adj. +N： constant...　持續努力

collaborative / joint...　共同努力

every...　全力

Elbow：肘部

1. V+N： bend / lift / raise one's...　縱飲

jog sb.'s...　輕推某人肘部以引起注意

lean / rest one's... on the table　把胳膊放在桌上

Election：選舉

1. V+N： fix / rig an...　在選舉中作弊

hold / schedule an...　舉行選舉

2. Adj.+N： a close / hotly contested...　競爭激烈的選舉

a general...　大（普）選

an off – year...　美國的期中選舉

a preliminary...　初選

a rigged...　作弊的選舉

Electricity：電

1. V+N： conduct...　導電

cut off...　斷電

generate...　發電

turn on...　打開電源

2. Adj.+N： frictional...　摩擦電

negative...　負（陰）電

positive...　正（陽電）

Element：元素、成分

1. Adj.+N： a basic / essential / vital...　重要成分

an extremist...　極端分子

foreign...　外國團體

the four... s　四元素（土、氣、火、水）

a subversive...　破壞分子

Embargo：禁運

1. V+N： lay / place / put an... on　對……實行禁運

lift / raise / remove the... on　對……解禁

Embarrassment：困窘

1. V+N： cause...　引起困窘

ease sb.'s...　紓緩某人的困窘

feel...　感到困窘

Emergency：緊急狀況

1. V+N： cause /create an...　引發緊急狀況

declare a state of...　宣布緊急狀況

2. Adj.+N： a grave / serious...　嚴重的緊急事件

a life – and – death...　生死攸關的緊急事件

declare a national...　宣布全國進入緊急狀況

Emotion：情感

1. V+N： express / show...　表達情感

stir up / whip up...　激起感情

2. Adj.+N： conflicting... s 矛盾的心情

mixed... s 複雜的心情

deep / sincere... 真摯的情感

pent – up... 鬱積的情感

Emphasis：強調

1. V+N： lay / place / put... on 強調

Employee：官員、員工

1. V+N： engage / hire / take on an... 僱用員工

dismiss / fire an... 解雇員工

2. Adj.+N： a government... 公務員

a white-collar... 白領員工

Era：年代、紀元

1. Adj.+N： the Christian / common... 公元

Error：錯誤

1. V+N： admit to (marking) an... 承認錯誤

commit / make an... 犯錯

correct... 修正錯誤

2. Adj.+N： a flagrant / glaring / serious... 嚴重錯誤

a printer's... 印刷錯誤

Escape：逃脫

1. V+N： have / make an... 逃走

organize an... 設計逃亡

thwart an... 阻撓逃亡

2. Adj.+N： afire... 太平梯 [門]

have a hairbreadth / narrow... 死裏逃生

Estate：房地產

1. V+N： administer / manage an... 經營地產

2. Adj.+N： personal... 動產

real... 房地產

Esteem：尊敬

1. V+N： command sb.'s... 博得某人尊敬

get the... of sb. 受到某人尊敬

hold sb. in high... 非常尊敬某人

2. Adj.+N： be held in great / high... 非常受尊敬

Estimate：預估

1. V+N： give / make an... 做估計

2. Adj.+N： a(n) approximate / rough... 粗略估計

a preliminary... 初步估計

Event：事件

1. V+N： celebrate an... 慶祝某件事

commemorate / mark an... 紀念某件事

2. N+V： An... occurs / takes place. 發生某件事

3. Adj.+N： a disastrous / tragic... 悲傷事件

an epoch-making... 畫時代的大事

Evidence：證據

1. V+N： dig up / turn up / unearth... 發掘（尋找）證據

furnish / produce / provide... 提供證據

gather... 蒐集證據

2. Adj.+N： ample... 充分證據

circumstantial... 間接證據

collateral... 旁證

concrete / hard... 具體證據

direct... 直接證據

documentary...　書面證據

material...　物證

oral / parole...　口頭證據

Evil：邪惡

1. V+N：　　　do... s　做壞事

overcome an...　戰勝邪惡

Exchange：交換、交流

1. Adj.+N：　　a cultural...　文化交流

foreign...　外匯

a frank... of views　坦承交換意見

a post...　福利社（簡稱PX）

Excitement：興奮

1. V+N：　　　arouse / cause / create / stir up...　引起騷動

feel...　感到興奮

2. Adj.+N：　　considerable / great / intense...　極大的興奮（騷動）

emotional...　情緒激動

Exhibition：展覽

1. V+N：   give / have / hold an...   舉辦展覽

2. Adj.+N：   an art...   藝術展覽

                       a trade...   商展

Existence ：存在、生活、生存方式

1. Adj.+N：   future...   來世

                       lead a hand-to-mouth...   勉強過活

                       miserable...   悲傷的生活

Expectations：期望

1. V+N：   answer / come up to / meet one's...   符合某人期望

                       entertain great...   抱很大期望

                       exceed / surpass one's...   超出某人期望

                       fall short of one's...   辜負某人期望

Expense：花費

1. V+N：   curb / curtail cut down on / reduce... s   減少費用

                       incur / run up a great...   花費很多

                       reimburse... s   償還費用

Extension：延期、延伸部

1. V+N：   ask for / request an... 　請求延期

                 get / receive an... 　獲得延期

                 give / grant an... 　給（准）予延期

2. Adj.+N：   business... 　分店

                 phone... 　電話分機

Extra ：額外的

1. V+N：   issue / publish / put out an... 　出號外

Facilities：設施

1. Adj.+N：   educational... 　教育設施

                 public... 　公共設施

                 recreational... 　娛樂設施

                 research... 　研究設備

                 transportation... 　交通設施

Fact：事實

1. V+N：   distort / twist (the)... s 　扭曲事實

Factory：工廠

1. V+N： close a... 關閉工廠

    manage / operate a... 經營工廠

    open a... 開工廠

Faint：昏迷

1. V+N： fall down in a... / fall into a... 昏倒

Faith：信心

1. V+N： have... in / place one's... in 相信，信任

    Lose... in 對……失去信心

2. Adj.+N： abiding/enduring/steadfast/strong/unshakable... 堅定的信心

Fan：扇子、迷

1. V+N： furl a... 折櫳扇子

    turn off a... 關電扇

    turn on a... 開電扇

    unfurl a... 打開扇子

    wave a... 搖扇子

2. Adj+N： a baseball... 棒球迷

    a ceiling... 吊扇

an electric...　電風扇

a film / movie / screen...　影迷

a ventilating...　通風機

Farm：農場

1. V+N：　　　　manage / operate / run / work a　經營農場

2. Adj+N：　　　a chicken...　養雞場

a dairy...　酪農場

a poultry...　家禽飼養場

a truck...　蔬菜農場

Farming：耕作

1. V+N：　　　　be engaged in...　務農

Fashion：時尚

1. V+N：　　　　come into...　流行

follow the...　迎合時尚

go out of...　過時、變爲不流行

set a...　創流行時尚

Fault：失誤

1. Adj.+N：　　　　a common...　常見的錯誤

　　　　　　　　　double...　（網球）兩次發球失誤

　　　　　　　　　a grave...　嚴重的過失

Favor：恩惠

1. V+N：　　　　do/grant (sb.)a...　幫（某人）忙

Fear：害怕、懼怕

1. V+N：　　　　arouse/inspire/kindle...　引起恐懼

　　　　　　　　　conquer...　克服恐懼

　　　　　　　　　feel...　感到害怕

2. Adj+N：　　　　groundless...　無緣由的恐懼

　　　　　　　　　linger-ing...　餘悸

Feast：宴會

1. V+N：　　　　give/make a...　設宴、舉行宴會

2. Adj.+N：　　　　a royal/sumptuous...　豐盛的宴會

Fever：熱度、興趣

1. V+N：　　　　abort a...　止熱

allay / bring down / shake off one's...　使退燒

catch / come down with / develop / have / run　a...　發燒

2. N+ V.：　　　A... abates / subsides.　發燒不退

3. Adj.+N：　　a continual / lingering...　持續不退的發燒

hayInterest　興趣

(1)　V+N：arouse/generate...　引發興趣

lose...　失去興趣

(2)　Adj.+N：deep/keen/profound...　極大興趣

Fight：格鬥

1. V+N：　　　pick / provoke / start a... with sb.　向某人尋釁格鬥

Figure：角色、人物

1. V+N：　　　cut a conspicuous...　露投角

cut a fine...　給人好印象

cut a poor / sorry...　露窮酸相

2. Adj.+N：　　a public...　公眾人物

Fine：罰款

1. V+N：　　　impose / levy a... on sb.　處某人罰金

incur a... of ten dollars　招致十元罰款

pay a...　付罰款

223

2. Adj.+N： a heavy / severe / stiff... 高額罰金

a mandatory... 強制罰款

3. N+Prep： a... for illegal 違規停車罰款

Fitting：裝置、配備

1. V+N： go for a... 試穿衣物

2. Adj.+N： electric... s 電器裝置

interior... s 室內設備

office... s 辦公室設備

Fiction：小說

1. Adj. + N： detective... 偵探小說

modern... 現代小說

realistic... 寫實主義小說

romantic... 浪漫小說

Fidelity：忠貞

1. V+N： swear... to 向……宣誓忠貞

2. Adj.+N： high... 高度傳眞（簡稱 hi-fi）

Field：土地、場

1. V+N： plow / till / work a... 耕田

2. Adj.+N： a paddy / rice... 稻田

a playing... 運動場

Flashlight：手電筒

1. V+N： shine a... on 用手電筒照

turn on a... 打開手電筒

Flat：平坦、洩氣輪胎

1. V+N： change a... 換洩氣輪胎

fix a... 修補洩氣輪胎

have a... 輪胎洩氣

Flexibility：柔軟度

1. V+N： demonstrate / show... 有彈性（適應性）

Flight：飛行

1. V+N： make / take a... 飛行

2. Adj.+N： a chartered 包機的飛行

a direct 直飛

a long-distance...　長途飛行

a nonstop...　不著陸飛行

Footstep：腳印

1. V+N：　　　dog the... s of sb.　尾隨某人

identify... s　鑑定腳印

recognize... s　辨認腳印

Forecast：預報、預測

1. V+N：　　　give / make a...　作預測

hazard a...　無把握地預測，姑且預測

2. Adj.+N：　　weather...　天氣預報

Forehead：前額

1. V+N：　　　knit / wrinkle (up) one's...　皺起前額

mop/wipe one's...　擦拭額頭（上的汗水）

2. Adj.+N：　　abroad / large...　寬闊的額頭

a furrowed / wrinkled...　起皺紋的前額

a high...　高額頭

a prominent...　凸出的前額

Foresight：遠見

1. V+N：　　　　　have...　有遠見

　　　　　　　　　lack...　缺乏遠見

Fortune：財富

1. V+N：　　　　　accumulate / amass / build up a...　積聚財富

　　　　　　　　　come into / inherit a...　繼承財產

　　　　　　　　　dissipate / squander one's...　揮霍財產

　　　　　　　　　make a...　發財

　　　　　　　　　seek one's...　離家闖天下

　　　　　　　　　tell sb.'s...　給某人算命

2. Adj.+N：　　　　be in good...　運氣好

　　　　　　　　　be in bad...　運氣壞

Foul：犯規

1. V+N：　　　　　claim a...　指出對方犯規

　　　　　　　　　commit a...　犯規

　　　　　　　　　play sb... .　以犯規動作對待某人

2. V+ Adv.：　　　……（比賽）犯規過多而被罰退場

3. Adj.+N：　　　　a personal...　侵人犯規

　　　　　　　　　a technical...　技術犯規

Foundation：基礎

1. V+N：　　　　　build up / lay the... of...　給……打基礎

Fowl：家禽、野鳥

1. V+N：　　　　　bread / keep / raise... s　飼養家禽

2. Adj.+N：　　　　table... s　食用家禽

　　　　　　　　　　a water...　水鳥

　　　　　　　　　　a wild...　野鳥

Freedom：自由

1. V+N：　　　　　enjoy...　享受自由

　　　　　　　　　　long for...　渴望自由

　　　　　　　　　　regain / win back one's...　重獲自由

2. Adj.+N：　　　　academic...　學術自由

　　　　　　　　　　the Four Freedoms... of worship, ... from want,... form fear

　　　　　　　　　　四大自由－言論自由，信仰自由，免於匱乏，免於恐懼

　　　　　　　　　　press...　出版自由

Friendship：友誼

1. V+N：　　　　　acquire the... of sb.　獲得某人的友誼

　　　　　　　　　　break……with sb.　與某人斷交

build up / establish the... between...　建立……之間的友誼

cultivate... with sb.　培養與某人的友誼

treasure / value...　珍惜友誼

2. Adj.+N：　enduring / firm...　牢固的友誼

longstanding...　老交情

school...　同窗情誼

a warm...　熱烈的友情

Funeral：葬禮

1. V+N：　attend a...　參加葬禮

conduct / hold a...　舉行葬禮

Furnish：陳設、布置

1. Adv.+Adj.：　an artistically... ed room　布置得很有美感的房間

an elegantly / tastefully... ed room　布置的很優雅的房間

a luxuriously... ed room　布置的很豪華的房間

a plainly / simply... ed room　陳設簡單的房間

Future：未來

1. V+N：　have a great...　前途遠大

map out / plan one's...　籌劃未來

2. Adj.+N： a bright / glorious / rosy...　光明的前途

a dark / dim...　黯淡的前途

Gain：獲得、利益

1. Adj.+N： illgotten... s　不義之財

illicit...　非法所得

a net...　淨利

2. Prep.+N： ... by five minutes　快五分

a... in weight　體重增加

Gale：強風

1. V+N： a... blows　強風吹

a... rages　強風肆虐

2. Adj.+N： a heavy / raging / sever...　一陣強風

Gap：缺口

1. V+N： bridge / close / fill / stop / supply a...　補缺

leave/make a...　遺留鴻溝

2. Adj.+N： a communications...　溝通鴻溝

a generation...　代溝

Gather：聚集

1. V+N：   ... the brows   皺眉

                       ... breath   喘口氣

                       ... one's senses   聚精會神

Generosity：慷慨

1. V+N：   demonstrate / show...   表現慷慨

2. Adj.+N：   lavish / magnanimous...   非常慷慨

Genius：天分

1. V+N：   display / show...   顯現天分

2. Adj.+N：   an artistic...   藝術天才

                       an inventive...   發明天才

                       latent...   潛在天才

                       rare...   稀有天才

Gesture：姿勢

1. V+N：   give / make a...   做手勢

                       use...   使用手勢

2. Adj.+N： a friendly...　友誼態度

human/kind...　慈悲態度

imperious...　傲慢姿態

Glance：一瞥

1. V+N： cast / dart / shoot / take... at sb.　看某人一眼

steal a... at sb.　偷窺某人一眼

2. Adj.+N： a casual / cursory / fleeting / passing...　匆匆一眼

Glory：榮耀

1. V+N： achieve / win...　獲得榮耀

bring... to sb.　帶給某人榮耀

2. Adj.+N： eternal / everlasting...　永恆榮耀

Goal：目標

1. V+N： achieve / attain / reach / realize a...　達成目標

set a...　設定目標

2. Adj.+N： a common...　共同目標

English
Technical
Articles

Goods：物品、商品

1. Adj.+N： capitial...　資本財

consumer...　消耗品

durable...　耐久財

Gossip：閒話

1. V+N： retail / spread...　散佈謠言

talk...　閒聊

2. Adj.+N： idle...　閒聊

malicious...　惡毒閒話

Grade：分數

1. V+N： get / receive a...　得分

make the...　成功、及格

2. Adj.+N： a failing...　不及格分數

a fair / mediore...　中等分數

a passing...　及格分數

Grant：補助金

1. V+N： award / give a...　給予補助金

get/obtain a... 獲得補助金

2. Adj.+N： a cash... 現金補助

a federal... 政府補助金

a research... 研究補助金

Grasp：瞭解

1. Adj.+N： a complete/ through... of... 對……徹底瞭解

a fundamental... 基本瞭解

a profound... 深刻瞭解

Gratitude：感激

1. V+N： deserve / merit one's... 值得某人感激

express / show... 表示感激

2. Adj.+N： deep / profound / unbounded 深切感激

sincere / heartfelt... 眞誠感激

Greeting：問候

1. V+N： extend / send... s to sb. 向某人問候

2. Adj.+N： a cordial / sincere / warm... 熱烈問候

Grief：悲痛

1. V+N：　　　　　assuage sb's...　減輕某人悲痛

　　　　　　　　　turn... into strenth　化悲痛爲力量

2. Adj.+N：　　　　bitter / profound...　深切悲痛

Groan：呻吟

1. V+N：　　　　　emit/ulter a...　發出呻吟

2. Adj.+N：　　　　an agonizing / a bitter...　痛苦呻吟

Growth：成長

1. V+N：　　　　　accelerate...　加速成長

　　　　　　　　　foster / promote...　促進成長

　　　　　　　　　hamper / retard / stunt...　阻礙成長

2. Adj.+N：　　　　mental...　智力發展

　　　　　　　　　rapid...　快速成長

　　　　　　　　　zero...　零成長

Guarantee：擔保

1. V+N：　　　　　give / offer / provide a...　提供擔保

2. Adj.+N：　　　　an effective...　有效保證

　　　　　　　　　a flimsy...　不可靠擔保

Guard：警衛

1. V+N： call out the... 呼叫警衛

post the... 布置警衛

2. Adj.+N： an honor... 儀隊

a life... 救生員

Guess：猜測

1. V+N： give / make a... 猜測

miss one's... 沒猜中

2. Adj.+N： a lucky... 幸運猜中

a random / wild... 瞎猜

Guide：導引

1. Adj.+N： a buying... 購買指南

a tourist... 導遊

a travelers'... 旅行指南

Halt：停止

1. V+N： bring to a... 使停止

call a... 命令停止

come to a... 停止

2. Adj.+N： a grinding / screeching...　軋然停止

a sudden...　徒然停止

Heritage：遺產

1. V+N： cherish one's...　珍視遺產

uphold one's...　維護傳統

2. Adj.+N： a splendid cultural...　輝煌的文化遺產

Hesitation：猶豫

1. V+N： feel some...　有點猶豫

show...　顯得猶豫

Ideal：理想

1. V+N： attain an...　達成理想

fulfill / realize high... S　實現崇高理想

Ignorance：無知

1. V+N： betray one's...　暴露某人的無知

feign / pretend... about　假裝不知道……

2. Adj.+N： profound / total... 徹底無知

Illusion：幻想

1. V+N： cherish/harbor an... 存著幻想

create / produce... 產生幻想

Immunity：免疫

1. V+N： acquire / develop... 獲得免疫

enjoy / gain... from conscription 免除兵役

2. Adj.+N： acquired... 後天免疫

natural... 先天免疫

diplomatic... 外交豁免權

Impact：影響

1. V+N： have / make great... on 對……產生大影響

Implement：實施、器具

1. V+N： ... a plan 實施計畫

2. Adj.+N： farm... s 農具

kitchen... s 廚房器具

Incentive：誘因

1. V+N： give / provide...　給予激勵

2. Adj.+N： a powerful / strong...　強烈誘因

Infection：感染

1. V+N： prevent...　預防感染

spread / transmit...　傳播感染

2. Adj.+N： contagious...　傳染性感染

a latent...　潛伏性感染

Inflation：通貨膨脹

1. V+N： check/control/curb...　抑制通貨膨脹

2. Adj.+N： double-digit...　兩位數通貨膨脹

Ingenuity：智巧

1. V+N： display / show...　顯現智巧

exercise / exert...　運用智巧

Inspection：調查

1. V+N： carry out / conduct...　調查

2. Adj.+N： a close / thorough...　詳細調查

Inspiration：靈感

1. V+N：   derive / draw... from   獲取靈感

Invasion：侵略

1. V+N：   launch an...   發動侵略

              make an... on   侵略

              repel / repulse an...   擊退侵略

Irritation：激怒

1. V+N：   allay / relieve...   減輕疼痛

              feel... = be irritated with   感到激怒

Issue：發行物、議題

1. V+N：   bring out / publish a new...   出版新期刊

              bring up / raise an...   提供議題

2. Adj.+N：   a back...   過期發行物

              a burning...   迫切議題

              a divisive...   造成紛爭議題

              a side...   次要議題

Jealousy：妒忌

1. V+N：　　　　arouse...　引起妒忌

display / exhibit / show... of sb.　表現出對某人的妒忌

2. Adj.+N：　　　burning / fierce...　強烈的妒忌

a lover's...　吃醋

Journey：旅程

1. V+N：　　　　cheat the...　排遣旅途

map out / plan a...　規劃旅途

2. Adj.+N：　　　a wedding...　新婚旅程

life's...　人生旅程

a pleasant...　愉快旅程

Justice：正義

1. V+N：　　　　administer / dispense...　執法

uphold...　高舉正義

2. Adj.+N：　　　social... 社會正義

Key：鑰匙

1. V+N：　　　　afford / furnish / offer the... to...　給……提供線索

duplicate a...　複製鑰匙

make a...　製造鑰匙

2. Adj.+N：　a golden... / a master / skeleton...　萬能鑰匙

Lawsuit：起訴

1. V+N：　bring / file a... against　對某人起訴

　　　　　lose a...　敗訴

　　　　　Win a...　勝

Leave：離開、假

1. V+N：　ask for...　請假

2. Adj.+N：　a sick...　病假

　　　　　a maternity...　產假

Leisure：閒暇

1. V+N：　Employ one's...　利用閒暇

　　　　　find... to do sth.　找出閒暇做事

2. Adj.+N：　a life of easy...　安逸的人生

Lesson：功課

1. V+N：　do one's lessons　做功課

dodge a...　逃課

neglect one's... s　荒廢功課

Lodging：住宿

1. V+N：　provide board and...　提供膳宿

share... s with　與……一起住宿

Take up one's...　投宿

Loyalty：忠誠

1. V+N：　pledge one's... to　發誓對……忠誠

Unshakable / unswerving...　不會動搖的忠誠

Manuscript：手稿、原稿

1. V+N：　polish...　潤稿

proofread...　校稿

reject a...　退稿

Mark：分數、記號

1. V+N：　attain/earn/gain high... s　得高分

give sb. full... s　給某人滿分

score 80... s　得八十分

Materral：材料、資料

1. V+N： assemble/collect/gather...　收集資料

2. Adj+N： printed... /matter　印刷品

reading...　讀物

research...　研究資料

teaching... s　教材

Meal：餐

1. V+N： cook one's... s　自己煮飯

fix/prepare a...　備餐

serve a...　上菜

2. Adj+N： a big/full/fenerous/substantial/sumptuous...　豐盛的一餐

a heavy...　飽餐一頓

a light...　便餐

a simple/spare...　簡餐

Mercy：憐憫、寬恕

1. V+N： beg the... of sb.　懇求某人寬恕

have... on/show... to sb.　憐憫某人

Miracle：奇蹟

1. Adj+N：   accomplish/do/perform/work a...   創造奇蹟

Mistake：錯誤、過失

1. Adj+N：   admit a...   承認錯誤

                 avoid a...   避免錯誤

                 commit/make/perpetrate a...   犯錯

Morals：風氣

1. Adj+N：   improve public...   改善社會風氣

                 protect/safeguard public...   維護社會風氣

Nature：自然

1. Adj+N：   betray/reveal one's true...   暴露某人的本性

                 congure...   征服自然

2. Adj+N：   Dame/Mother Nature   大自然

                 human...   人性

                 the rational...   理性

                 second...   第二天性

······To Be Continued······

☆ 讀者心得增補筆記欄 ☆

截至2005年編者發表的期刊論文

編者楊勝安博士 (Yang, Sheng-An) 所發表的期刊論文（2005年為止）

1. Yang, Sheng-An and Chen, Cha'o-Kuang, "Magnetohydrodynamic Effects upon Momentum Transfer on a Continuously Moving Flat Plate," Computers Mathematics Application, Vol.23, No.10, pp.27-33, 1992, SCI.

2. Yang, Sheng-An and Chen, Cha'O-Kuang, "Laminar Film Condensation on a Finite-size Horizontal Plate," J.CSME, Vol.13, No. 2, pp.128-131, 1992. (EI)

3. Yang, Sheng-An and Chen, Cha'O-Kuang, "Laminar Film Condensation on a Finite-size Horizontal Plate with Suction at the Wall," Applied Math. Modelling, Vol.16, pp.325-329, Jun.1992. (SCI, EI)

4. Yang, S.-A and Chen, C.K., "Filmwise condensation on Nonisother-mal Horizontal Elliptical Tube with Surface tension," AIAA J. of Thermo-physics & Heat Transfer 7. No.4, pp.729-732, 1993. (SCI, EI)

5. Yang, Sheng-An and Chen, C.K., "Effects of Surface Tension and Noniso-thermal Wall Temperature Variation upon Filmwise Condensation on Vertical Ellipsoids/sphere," Proc. Royal Society Lond A: 442, 301-312, 1993. (EI, SCI)

6. Yang, Sheng-An and Chen, C.K., "Laminar Film Condensation on a Hori-zontal Elliptical Tube with Uniform Surface Heat Flux and Suction at the

Porous Wall," J. CSME,Vol.14, No.1, pp.93-100, 1993. (EI)

7. Yang, Sheng-An and Chen, Cha'O-Kuang,"Transient film condensation on a horizontal elliptical tube,"J. Phys-D,Vol.26, pp.793-797, 1993. (SCI, EI)

8. Yang, Sheng-An and Chen,C.K., "Role of Surface Tension and Ellipticity in Laminar Film Condensation on Horizontal Elliptical Tube," Int. J. Heat & Mass Transfer.,Vol.36, No.12, pp.3135-3141, 1993. (國科會甲等獎- SCI, EI)

9. Yang, S.-A and Chen C.K.,"Laminar Film Condensation on a Horizontal Elliptical Tube with Variable Wall Temperature," ASME J. Heat Transfer 116, 1046-1049, 1994 .(SCI, EI)

10. Chen,C.K., and Yang, S.-A, "Laminar Film condensation inside a Horizontal Elliptical Tube with Variable wall Temperature," Int. J. Heat & Fluid Flow, 15, No. 1, 75-78, 1994 (SCI, EI)

11. Chiou. J. S., Yang, S.-A, and Chen. C.K.,"Laminar film Condensation inside a Horizontal Elliptical Tube," Applied Math. Modelling, Vol. 18, 340-346, 1994. (SCI, EI)

12. Chiou, J. S.; Yang, S.-A and Chen,C.K., "Filmwise Condensation on a Horizontal Elliptical Tube embedded in Porous Media," Chemical Eng. Communication, Vol. 127, 125-135, 1994. (SCI, EI)

13. Hsu, C. H., and Yang, S.-A,"Mixed-Convection Film Condensation from Downward Flowing Vapors onto a Sphere with Variable Wall Temperature," Heat and Mass Transfer, Vol. 33, pp.85-91,1997, (SCI, EI)

14. Yang, S.-A and Hsu, C. H., "Mixed-convection Film Condensation on a Horizontal Elliptical Tube with Uniform Surface Heat Flux," Numerical Heat Transfer, Part A,Vol. 32, pp. 85-95, 1997. (SCI, EI)

15. Hsu, C. H., and Yang, S.-A, "Mixed-Convection Film Condensation from Downward Flowing Vapors onto a Sphere with Uniform Wall Heat Flux," Heat and Mass Transfer, Vol. 32, pp.385-391, 1997. (SCI, EI)

16. Yang, S.-A, "Superheated Laminar Film Condensation on a Non-isothermal Horizontal Tube," AIAA, J. of Thermophysics and Heat Transfer, Vol. 11, No.4, pp.526-532, 1997. (SCI, EI)

17. Yang, S. -A and Hsu, C. H., "Superheated Mixed-Convection Film Condensation in the Forward Region of s Cylinder or Sphere," J.CSME, Vol. 18, No. 1, pp.85-93, 1997. (EI)

18. Yang, S.-A and Hsu, C. H., "Filmwise Condensation on a Vertical Porous Ellipsoid with Uniform Suction Velocity," Chem. Eng. Communication,Vol.160, pp.123-135, 1997. (SCI,EI)

19. Yang, S. -A and Hsu, C. H., "Free and Forced Convection Film

Condensation form a Horizontal Elliptical Tube with a Vertical Plate and Horizontal Tube as Special Cases," Int. J. Heat and Fluid Flow, Vol.18, pp.567-574, 1997. (SCI, EI)

20. Hsu, C. H. and Yang, S.-A, "Pressure Gradient and Variable Wall Temperature Effects during Filmwise Condensation from Downward Flowing Vapors onto a Horizontal Tube," Int .J. Heat and Mass Transfer, Vol.42, pp.2419-2426, 1999. (SCI, EI)

21. Yang, S.-A, and Hsu, C. H., "Mixed-Convection Film Condensation on a Horizontal Elliptical Tube with Variable Wall Temperature," J. of the CSME, Vol.20, No.4, pp.373-384, 1999. (EI)

22. Lin, Yan-Ting and Yang, Sheng-An "Turbulent Film Condensation on a Horizontal Elliptical Tube with Variable Wall Temperature," J. of Marine and Ocean Science, Vol. 12, No. 4, 300-308, 2004. (EI)

23. Yang, Sheng-An and Lin, Yan-Ting "Turbulent Film Condensation on a Horizontal Elliptical Tube," Heat and Mass Transfer, Vol.41, pp.495-502, 2005 (SCI, EI)

24. Yang, Sheng-An, and Lin, Yan-Ting, "Turbulent Film Condensation on a Non-isothermal Horizontal Tube-Effect of Eddy Diffusivity," Applied Math. Modelling, 29, pp.1149-1163, 2005. (SCI, EI)

25. Lin, Yan-Ting and Yang, Sheng-An "Turbulent Film Condensation on a Nonisothermal Horizontal Tube," J. of Mechanics, Vol. 21, No.4, pp.171-178, 2005. (SCI, EI)

26. Yang, Sheng-An; Lee, Jung -Yu and Yang, Wen-Jei "Numerical Visulization of Turbulent Filing Boiling Heat Transfer And Vapor Film Growth on Horizontal Elliptical Tubes," Journal of Flow Visualization and Image Processing, Vol.1, pp.1-14, 2005. (EI)

27. Lee, J. Y. and Yang, S.-A "An Analysis of Free Convection Turbulent Film Boiling on a Horizontal Elliptical Tube", Journal of Chinese Society Mechanical Engineering, accepted, 2005. (EI)

28. Lee, G. C. and Yang, S.-A "Laminar Film Condensation on an Inclined Elliptical Tube", J. of KUAS, Vol. 34 , pp.175-182, 2005.

29. Li, Guan-Cyun and Yang, Sheng-An "Thermodynamic Analysis of Free Convection Film Condensation on an Elliptical cylinder," J. of The Chinese Institute Engineers, accepted in 2005. (to appear in 2006) (SCI, EI)

30. Dung, S. C. and Yang, S.-A "Second Law Based Optimization of Free Condensation Film-Wise Condensation on Horizontal Tube, " Int. Comm. Heat and Mass Transfer, accepted in 2005. (to appear in 2006) (SCI, EI)

English
Technical
Articles

31. Dung, S. C.; Dung, S. H. Tzeng, and Yang, S.-A., "Entropy Generation of Free Convection Film Condensation from Downward Flowing Vapors onto a Cylinder or Sphere," Journal of Mechanics, revised in 2005. (to appear in 2006) (SCI, EI)

32. Tzeng, S. H. and Yang, S.-A "Second Law Analysis and Optimization for Film-wise Condensation from Downward Flowing Vapors onto a Sphere," Submit to Heat and Mass Transfer, 2005. (SCI,EI)

33. Li, G. C. and Yang, S.-A. "Entropy Generation Minimization of Free Convection Film Condensation on an Elliptical Cylinder," Submit to Int. J. Heat and Fluid Flow, 2005. (SCI, EI)

研討會論文

1. 楊勝安，「表面張力對橢圓球之膜狀凝結影響研究」，第八屆技術及職業教育研討會，pp.20 - 39，1993。

2. Yang, S.-A., "Mixed-Convection Film Condensation from Downward Flowing Vapors onto a Porous Horizontal Tube with Uniform Suction Velocity, " Proc. of the 13th National Conference of CSME, Taipei, pp.324-329, 1996.

3. Yang, S.-A, and Hsu, C. H., "Free Convection Film Boiling on a Vertical Ellipsoid, " Proc. of the 2nd National Conference of Chinese Military Academy for 75th anniversary , Feng Shan, 1998.

4. 林彥廷、楊勝安「水平橢圓管外受向下漏流飽和蒸汽流動之膜狀凝結分析」第二十一屆中國機械工程學會研討會，國立中山大學，2004.

5. 楊勝安，「平行均勻流場內等速移動平板之熱傳分析」第五屆技術及職業教育研討會，pp.4231 - 4239，1990。

6. 楊勝安，「多孔隙流體可滲透性流平板之熱對流」第五屆技職教育研討會，pp. 4221 - 4230，1990。

7. 楊勝安，「非等溫球面上膜狀凝結熱傳研究」，第八屆技職研討會，Mar. 1993。

8. Yang, Sheng-An and Lin, Yan-Ting, "Effect of Eddy Diffusivity on Turbulent Film Condensation Outside a Horizontal Tube," 4th International Conference on Transoprt Phenomena in Multiphase Systems, Poland June 26-30, 2005.

9. Lee, J. Y. and Yang, S.-A., "Free convection turbulent film boiling on a horizontal cylinder including eddy diffusivity effect," AASRC/CCAS Joint Conference, C8, 5, 2004.

10. Yang, Sheng-An; Lee, Jung -Yu and Yang, Wen-Jei, "Turbulent Film Boiling on a Horizontal elliptical tubes," The 5th Pacific Symposium on Flow Visualization and Image Processing, PSFVIP-5-230, 2005.

11. Li, G. C. and Yang, S.-A., "Laminar Film Condensation on an Inclined Elliptical Cylinder with Variable Wall Temperature," 22nd CSME Conference, A8-024, NCU, 2005.

12. Li, G. C. and Yang, S.-A., "An Analysis of Influencing Laminar Film Condensation Heat Transfer Characteristics on an Inclined Elliptical Tube by Taguchi Method", 22nd CSME Conference, A8-005, NCU, 2005.

13. Dung, S. C. and Yang, S.-A., "Entropy Generation of Laminar Film Condensation on a Horizontal Tube.", The 29th National Conference on Theoretical and Applied Mechanics, A028, December 16-17, 2005, NTHU, Hsinchu, Taiwan.

14. Tzeng, S. H. and Yang, S.-A., "Entropy Generation of Free Convection Film Condensation from Downward Flowing Vapors onto a Sphere," The 29th National Conference on Theoretical and Applied Mechanics, A027, December 16-17, 2005, NTHU, Hsinchu, Taiwan.

翻譯過的大學教科書

1. "Vector Mechanics for Engineers" Dymanics, F. P. Beer and E. R. Johnston Jr.3rd. Ed. (1999) McGraw-Hill；滄書局。

2. "Advanced Engineering Mathematics" E: Kreyzig, 9th Ed. (2005) John Wiley & Sons, Inc.,；歐亞書局。

English
Technical
Articles

95年榮獲研究金鐸獎後記

　　去年兼任模具系主任與所長時，收到全國工業職業教育學會通知：技職教育體系推薦傑出研究人員角逐金鐸獎選拔。 個人由於近三年指導技職教育體系研究生發表十餘篇 SCI期刊論文，且篇篇均藉著筆者一開始編寫的科技英文論文便覽草稿來指導完成，於是應全華圖書公司林副總之邀，在去年三月正式出版。因此書之創新實用成效，獲得本校工學院推薦參與此一金鐸獎之角逐，很幸運竟脫穎而出，榮獲95年研究金鐸獎，感謝上帝再度施恩！

　　上學期筆者正式在模具系所開授「科技英文論文寫作」，計47位工學院與電資學院研究生來選修，除了對本書修訂有直接的幫助外，也因此編成教師上課用簡報。事實上，此簡報可當作教科書的補充教材，因為除了本書內容以外，筆者另編排一些英文法架構的教材與練習在此簡報中，盼對採用本書的教授先進有所助益，是幸！

于96年3月修訂

參考書目

1. 椛田義明，J. C. Mathes，2003年，「科技論文、報告的書面英文表現」，建興文化。

2. 廣岡慶彥，2004年，「理工人會議出席、留學研究科技英語會話大突破」，建興文化。

3. 崎村耕二，2003年，「英語論文寫作技巧」，眾文圖書。

4. Ted Knoy "English Oral Presentations for Chinese Technical Writers-A Case Study Approach" Ind. Tech. Research Inst., Union Chemical Lab, 1995.

5. "Oxford Advanced Learner's Dictionary of Current English." 4th ed. Oxford：Oxford University Press, 1989.

6. 楊景邁、簡清國、林茂竹，1992年，「建宏多功能英漢辭典」，建宏出版。

☆ 讀者心得增補筆記欄 ☆

國家圖書館出版品預行編目資料

一定要讓你發表得出去之英文科技論文便覽 ／
楊勝安編著. －－二版. －－臺北縣土城市：
全華圖書，2007〔民96〕
　　面；　公分
參考書目：面
ISBN　978-957-21-5887-6（平裝）
1. 科技英文－作文　2.論文寫作法
805.175　　　　　　　　　　　　　　96010162

一定要讓你發表得出去之
英文科技論文便覽
（第二版）

作　　者：楊勝安
美術編輯：余孟玟・柯瑾芸
封面設計：吳佳昀・游雅惠
發 行 人：陳本源
出 版 者：全華圖書股份有限公司
地　　址：236台北縣土城市忠義路21號
電　　話：02-2262-5666（總機）
傳　　真：02-2262-8333
郵政帳號：0100836-1號
印 刷 者：宏懋打字印刷股份有限公司
圖書編號：09063017
二版二刷：2009年10月
定　　價：新臺幣 320 元
I S B N：978-957-21-5887-6（平裝）

全華網路

hppt://www.opentech.com.tw
http://www.chwa.com.tw
book@chwa.com.tw

勘誤表

書　號			書　名		作　者
頁　數	行　數		錯誤或不當之詞句		建議修改之詞句

我有話要說：（其它之批評與建議，如封面、編排、內容、印刷品質等．．．．）

書友服務卡

填寫日期：　　　/　　　/

姓名：　　　　　　　　　生日：西元　　　年　　　月　　　日　性別：□男 □女

電話：（　　）　　　　　傳真：（　　）　　　　　手機：

e-mail：　　　　　　　　（必填）

註：數字零，請用 ⊘ 表示，數字 1 與英文 L 請另註明，謝謝！

通訊處：□□□□□

學歷：□博士 □碩士 □大學 □專科 □高中・職

職業：□工程師 □教師 □學生 □軍・公 □其他

學校／公司：　　　　　　　　　　　　　科系／部門：

・需求書類：

□A.電子 □B.電機 □C.計算機工程 □D.資訊 □E.機械 □F.汽車 □I.工管 □J.土木
□K.化工 □L.設計 □M.商管 □N.日文 □O.美容 □P.休閒 □Q.餐飲 □其他

本次購買圖書為：　　　　　　　　　　　　　　書號：

・您對本書的評價：

封面設計：□非常滿意 □滿意 □尚可 □需改善，請說明
內容表達：□非常滿意 □滿意 □尚可 □需改善，請說明
版面編排：□非常滿意 □滿意 □尚可 □需改善，請說明
印刷品質：□非常滿意 □滿意 □尚可 □需改善，請說明
書籍定價：□非常滿意 □滿意 □尚可 □需改善，請說明
整體滿意度：請說明

・您在何處購買本書？

□書局 □網路書店 □書展 □團購 □其他

・您購買本書的原因？（可複選）

□個人需要 □幫公司採購 □親友推薦 □老師指定之課本 □其他

・您希望全華以何種方式提供出版訊息及特惠活動？

□電子報 □DM □廣告（媒體名稱　　　　　　　　　）

・您是否上過全華網路書店？（www.opentech.com.tw）

□是 □否 您的建議：

・您希望全華出版那方面書籍？

・您希望全華加強那些服務？

~感謝您提供寶貴意見，全華將秉持服務的熱忱，出版更多好書，以饗讀者。

書友專屬網址：http://bookers.chwa.com.tw

全華網路書店 http://www.opentech.com.tw 客服信箱：service@chwa.com.tw

訂書專線：（02）2262-5666 分機 321-324　傳真：（02）2262-8333

◎請詳填、並書寫端正，謝謝！

98.05 450,000份

（請由此線剪下）

歡迎加入 全華書友 行列

廣 告 回 信
板橋郵局登記證
板橋廣字第540號

行銷企劃部 收

全華圖書股份有限公司
236 台北縣土城市忠義路21號